the ORIGINALS

The Resurrection

CREATED BY JULIE PLEC
based on the Vampire Diaries

the ORIGINALS

The Resurrection

www.HQNBooks.com

HQN™

www.HQNBooks.com

ISBN-13: 978-0-373-78891-0

THE ORIGINALS: THE RESURRECTION

An HQN Books novel/May 2015

Dear Reader:

Welcome back for the final book in the Originals series. If reveling in the dramatic lives of current-day Klaus, Elijah, and Rebekah Mikaelson on the CW isn't enough for you, don't worry—just turn the page to see where their stories began. Courtesy of HQN Books, in association with Alloy Entertainment, this trilogy explores the dark past of the Originals with brand-new tales.

In the last two books, you saw how far Klaus would go for love. In book three, *The Resurrection,* you'll understand how far he'll go for power. After establishing a joint rule with the werewolves, the Mikaelsons have governed in peace for the past twenty years. Except Klaus never wanted eternal harmony; he wanted the entire city to kneel before him, covered in the blood of his rivals. And now he might finally get his chance. With Elijah and Rebekah distracted by their own desires, Klaus seizes the opportunity to take the city for himself. But when a new enemy rises up from the shadows of New Orleans, the three siblings will have to join forces and fight with everything they have if they want to save their home.

In *The Originals: The Rise*, *The Loss*, and *The*

Resurrection, the Mikaelson vampires are examined in a whole new way. Turn the page for a book that has all the violence, forbidden love, and lust for power of the TV show, and a story that will satisfy your hunger for more.

With best wishes,
Julie Plec
Creator and Executive Producer of *The Originals*

PROLOGUE

March 21, 1788

*T*he city was burning. From the east end to the church, New Orleans was lit up with flames, and Klaus Mikaelson was to blame. José Pilón sat on a low hill, watching the only home he'd ever known vanish before his eyes. Smoke rose from the city and seeped into the bayou, billowing into dark, sooty clouds. The full moon was bright and glowed an ominous red as it hovered above the flames.

José was born into an unprecedented era of peace, but his death had heralded a new age of violence. The Mikaelsons just couldn't leave well enough alone. Any truce that involved the three Original vampires wasn't worth the paper it was written on, not in the long run.

Sooner or later, one of them would get angry, jealous, or just bored.

Nine times out of ten that "one" would be Niklaus, the most volatile of the three siblings. José had once believed he would be loyal to Klaus Mikaelson forever—that sharing a vampire's blood created an eternal link of brotherhood. But Klaus had lied. To suit his own purposes, the middle Mikaelson sibling had turned on his enemies and his friends alike, and now José's city was burning to the ground.

He was supposed to have burned with it.

José had been born with the skills of a thief, and this time he had stolen his life back. He'd spent his childhood moving unseen through the back alleys and crooked lanes of New Orleans, noticing what others ignored and taking what wasn't his. It had served him well—as a human and as a vampire.

After the fire had started to spread, panic followed. José had kept his head down, ignoring the chaos and thinking only of escape. The main door had been barred, but any good thief knew there was always more than one way out.

He bet his life that he could reach the river before the fire overtook its banks, wooden warehouses catching in a torrent of flames. José waited until the freight doors that opened onto the docks weakened and caved in.

He covered his mouth and nose so he wouldn't breathe in the smoke, and stayed low to the ground. Soon he was cut off from everyone, the others enveloped in the blaze. Their screams pierced through the deafening roar of the fire.

Once the warehouse collapsed under its own weight, José managed to slither out from under the fallen beams and throw himself into the river before his body fully caught flame. Burns would heal easy enough, but only if he could make it out alive.

He wasn't alone as he waded through the Mississippi River. Dozens of other citizens fled the city with only the clothes on their back, desperate to get to the other side of the bayou.

The smell of smoke burned in José's throat and he coughed up water as he dragged himself through the swamp and up the riverbank. Even from his spot on the bluffs, watching the fire reflect on the water below, José could feel the heat of the fire biting at his skin. The wind whipped sparks along the water, launching a thousand embers from one wooden roof to the next. The fire was traveling faster than any human could possibly stop it, and it was clear that by morning there would be nothing left of the city. It was the greatest fire New Orleans had ever seen—and would hopefully ever see again. They were safe until the next time

Klaus got angry, at least.

Klaus might have given him eternal life, but he had also tried to take it away again, and to José's way of thinking—taking an eye for an eye—that made them even. José was immortal and powerful, yet also homeless and penniless, an outcast with no place or purpose in the world. José wished he could help stop the destruction and eventually assist in the rebuild, but he knew he could never return. New Orleans was too dangerous for him now—Klaus would always be on the lookout for a deserter.

Still, he couldn't bring himself to turn his back on New Orleans just yet. He knew that he was witnessing more than the death of a city—it was the beginning of a resurrection, and it was a sight to behold. Whatever Klaus had meant to accomplish, this deadly blaze wasn't where the story ended. As soon as the embers cooled, New Orleans would rise again from the ashes, just as she always did.

ONE

A few weeks earlier . . .

"**D**rink!"

Dozens of voices picked up the command, turning it into a chant. "Drink," they all shouted at the thief. Everyone else had already taken their turn, pledging their allegiance to Klaus's army by drinking his blood. Klaus let them think the gesture was symbolic—what was the point in letting them all know they'd be vampires by the end of the night? That'd only result in an unnecessary struggle, and Klaus never did anything to make his life harder.

The energy in the room was at a steady thrum, and it felt as if the very blood in his veins vibrated with the cries of men. Klaus had outgrown the family mansion, shedding it in favor of a roomy four-story garrison in the center of town. It was a more fitting place for his new calling—a place of war.

There had to be a hundred new recruits in the large main hall, banging their tankards on the long wooden tables and shouting encouragement to the next victim. Klaus sat alone on a dais, where he had received each of his subjects in turn. One was a whore from the Southern Spot, the oldest brothel in New Orleans and, by Klaus's estimation, still the best. She'd run afoul of the madam and been thrown out. But she'd refused to go quietly—showing some real fire and a surprisingly creative vocabulary. Another was a bandit who'd been rounded up by the Spanish soldiers who patrolled the countryside—and who had handed him over to Klaus for a small fee. The youngest were a fresh crop of runaways who'd been discovered scavenging in one of Klaus's warehouses near the harbor. He'd convinced the teenagers that they'd have a much better life working for him than begging for scraps.

The last recruit to drink was the thief. José had been caught with one hand in the safe of the Southern Spot. The manager, a hothead whom Klaus suspected might be doing some skimming of his own, had wanted to kill the man and dump his body in the river. But Klaus had an eye for potential—he could spot those who were loyal. All Klaus needed to give him was a new life, a new family, and a new mission. That might have seemed like an impossible gift to give, but not for an Original vampire.

Drinking blood was a gruesome way to pledge allegiance, but the extreme nature of the hazing was a sure way to have volunteers begging to join Klaus's cause. Everyone in the hall understood that being a part of Klaus's army would require dangerous things. That was the appeal. And Klaus had no use for an army that wasn't ready to die for him.

It hadn't always been like this—his mad thirst for ultimate control and power. Klaus's past self would have traded the entire city for a life with Vivianne Lescheres, but he understood now that it was never meant to be. If he couldn't have her, he would rule New Orleans, and the werewolves—his "co-rulers" for the past twenty-two years—would consider themselves lucky if he stopped there. Without love, power was the only prize left that was worth fighting for . . . and, as it happened, Elijah himself was distracted by love at that very moment, finally giving Klaus the chance to take what was rightfully his.

If the gossip among the Southern Spot's laundresses was to be believed, Elijah was entertaining a little side romance. At the moment, Klaus didn't care who his brother spent his time with, as long as it kept Elijah out of his way. He was sure the tantalizing news would come in handy just when he needed it to, but for now, it was Klaus's little secret. Since his older brother couldn't fully dedicate himself to controlling their city, Klaus would do it—and he would do it in his own way, as he should have from the start. The werewolves were coming, and Klaus was determined to strike first and in force.

Peacetime was boring, anyway. Klaus had spent the last twenty years building his family's fortune to levels that rivaled a king's. He had become the foremost merchant in the city, and there was no trade route out of New Orleans that his ships didn't sail. He had risen as high as anyone could in a city at peace, and it still wasn't enough. Conquest was what Klaus was good at, what he was destined for. Everything else was just a distraction, and Klaus was done with those.

Fortunately, a new enemy had presented itself just when Klaus was ready to go looking for one. As if the werewolves' role in Vivianne's two deaths wasn't enough of an insult, they'd grown particularly bold in recent weeks. There had been daytime raids on the Mikaelsons' businesses, and frequent sneak attacks on their warehouses and ships. Now Guillaume, one of the humans whose eyes and ears Klaus relied on, informed him that the werewolves were poised to strike directly at the vampires themselves.

As part of a pact, Elijah had generously given the Collado wolves a foothold in the city, even after they had failed to stop an army of dead witches. And yet, instead of showing gratitude, the werewolves had spent the last two decades grasping for more and more. There was no reasoning with them, and the disastrous failure of Elijah's peaceful diplomacy was more than enough proof of that. As long as the vampires were forced to share and negotiate, true power would never be theirs. The only solution was to wipe out their rivals, as Klaus had wanted to do from the night he had first arrived on these shores.

Klaus stared down at the thief who knelt before him, ready to use compulsion if he tried to bolt. José had sharp, angular features, with a pointed nose, watchful blue eyes, and starkly black hair. He couldn't have been more than nineteen, and to Klaus's critical eye he didn't look like much. He didn't need to, though. Klaus had more than enough power to go around.

"Drink!" his soldiers shouted, and Klaus could see the thief's pulse beat in his throat. José lifted his shot glass and drained it in one swallow, the blood leaving an unsightly stain on his lips. He gagged a little as he tried to control his disgust at the taste of the thick, warm blood. Klaus could dimly remember feeling the same disdain, but centuries upon centuries as a vampire had cured him of that distaste.

Becoming a vampire was a cure for any number of life's ills.

The thief looked around uncertainly, awed by the thundering roar of approval that shook the hall. Klaus's army was in a merry mood that night, and it was only going to get better. Klaus studied the trembling man before him for a long moment. With a welcoming smile, he stepped forward and snapped José's neck, feeling the vertebrae pop under his fingers.

The room went silent, a hundred faces staring, mouths gaping open in shock. The dead man collapsed to the floor in an awkward heap, but Klaus didn't bother to watch him fall. Instead, he leapt forward, moving faster than human eyes could follow, reached for the neck of the nearest human, snapped it, and then seized the next.

There was barely time for the last man to scream—a thin, strangled sound that choked off when Klaus's hand closed around his windpipe. He took pleasure in killing the last man slowly, watching him struggle for air as the surrounding bodies thumped to the ground.

The whole ordeal was over in seconds. Klaus walked among his men and women, down along the narrow aisle that ran between the tables. They had all been criminals and deserters, lost until he had come along. Now they were an army of the dead.

Klaus was the only one of his siblings who seemed to realize that the only true safety lay in power. A better network, a bigger army, more resources, more weapons—there was no position too strong, in Klaus's opinion. The fact that Mikael hadn't come for them yet didn't mean he had ended his hunt. His children—and Klaus, his hated stepson—needed to be in the strongest position possible when Mikael appeared, and that meant the entire city should be under their control.

The last of the brisk winter air swept through the open courtyard and struck Klaus in the face. The night was promising; he could feel it. Klaus's vampire blood was already getting to work, changing and reforming the men and women, dragging them toward an entirely new kind of life. By the following night, he would have a hundred new vampires in his army, all of them fanatically loyal to Klaus and Klaus alone.

TWO

Rebekah inhaled the smell of damp earth as her horse cantered through the Louisiana countryside. It felt good to be out of the city, free of the confining walls of the mansion and away from the oppressive eyes of her brothers. She had, once upon a time, promised her siblings that they would remain together for eternity, but back then she'd had no idea just how long eternity could last.

"What a shame to let the horses have all the fun," Luc called to her. "We could just run ourselves."

Rebekah couldn't match his lightness of spirit, not until she'd dealt with a killer in the midst of her family—Klaus. She'd fled from New Orleans with an image of horror seared into her mind, and she wouldn't be free of it until Klaus paid for what he'd done.

Pulling her blonde hair back from her face, Rebekah longed to feel as free as Luc, who let the wind whip through his thick golden waves. It was his easy attitude toward life that had inspired her to invite him along, with the hope that some of his humor might pierce the gloom that had shrouded her ever since she'd found Marguerite Leroux's dead body in her bed.

"We're in no hurry," she countered, and Luc's blue eyes twinkled wickedly. In spite of everything that weighed on her, Rebekah couldn't look at him without either laughing or lusting . . . often both at once. She had definitely made the right choice of traveling companion. "The horses may be a bit slower than we are, but I don't want to risk any attention."

Even though it was the middle of the night, one never knew who might be watching. Elijah had intended to keep Klaus out of trouble by placing him in charge of New Orleans's booming trade business, but all that had accomplished was to give Klaus eyes and ears everywhere. He had become an absolute terror, full of increasingly nasty surprises. Marguerite's death was just the most recent example, but Klaus had threatened and terrorized the poor girl for years. He'd never fully forgiven Marguerite for what her mother, the witch Lily, had done to his beloved Vivianne.

Luc urged his horse on as they crested a low hill, and Rebekah kicked her own mare forward to keep pace. An emerald valley spread out below them, carpeted with lush grass and moonlight. A little village huddled at its far end, near a stream.

"We should stop here for daybreak," Rebekah suggested, feeling the stress of New Orleans, her family, and even poor Marguerite begin to fade just a little bit. "I'm sure there's an inn."

"I think I see one," Luc agreed, swinging down from his saddle. She did the same, falling in beside him. He wrapped a casual arm around her waist, running a finger along the boning of her corset. She relaxed into his hand with a sigh.

"Should I be expecting your brothers to drop in on us at any point, or will we be alone?" he asked, teasingly pulling at a silk bow on her hip.

Luc Benoit had been born east of the river in the newly minted United States, and it showed in everything he did. He had all the restless curiosity of an explorer, and the spontaneous confidence of a boy who had been raised to believe he could tackle any challenge that came his way. Wolves, bears, and whip-fast alligators had prowled the world around him, so he had never bothered with learning to fear the unknown.

That swaggering recklessness had eventually been his undoing, although Rebekah could tell it had taught him nothing whatsoever. Luc had fallen in with a gang of privateers, bullying the British along the northern coasts, and when that work was done he had simply kept on tormenting others for profit. He had become exactly the kind of shiftless troublemaker who Klaus was rounding up to form his ludicrous "army." In fact, Klaus had already recruited Luc when Rebekah had first met him.

She'd had no choice but to make Luc a vampire herself, saving him from a fate tied to Klaus's endless attempts at self-destruction. Her troubled brother always managed to destroy everyone around him, emerging unscathed again and again, and Luc was far too handsome to end up dead. At the time, Rebekah had thought she deserved a dashingly sexy distraction. Then Klaus had killed Marguerite, and everything had changed.

"I have lived and traveled with my brothers for centuries," she told Luc. "But this is a trip just for the two of us. I haven't been to this area in ages, and I need your help finding one particular thing." She couldn't promise that Klaus or Elijah wouldn't pursue them, as neither would be pleased with Rebekah's decision. But she and her loyal new lover had a good head start, and Rebekah knew how to disappear when she needed to.

She was done answering to her family. That had all been over the moment she had laid eyes on the bloody stake broken off in the center of Marguerite Leroux's thin chest. The lanky girl should have finished growing into a woman years ago, and she would have if Klaus hadn't accidentally killed her during the madness that had followed his foolhardy resurrection of Vivianne Lescheres. Rebekah had saved her, freezing her as a teenager forever . . . or at least until Klaus got it into his head to make good on some of his wild threats.

Klaus had always enjoyed using the vampires closest to his siblings as a means to control them. It hadn't taken him long to see that Rebekah felt a genuine bond with Marguerite, and he seemed to take particular pleasure in reminding Rebekah that he could destroy that connection in a single, violent moment. Even after Klaus had slaughtered two of the footmen for some imagined insult, Rebekah never believed he would take away someone she truly loved—not until she had seen the proof with her own eyes.

It was too cruel, too unfeeling, even for Klaus. But after Vivianne died, Klaus abandoned any of the decency left inside of him. His heart was shut off from anyone but himself. And so as Rebekah held Marguerite's cold body against her own, she had vowed that she would put an end to Klaus's misery once and for all.

"Your brothers don't know you've left," Luc guessed, watching her intently. His full lips pressed together thoughtfully. "Don't worry, Rebekah, I'm a man of my word. I can keep your secret."

He started to speak again, but Rebekah caught him by the shoulders to kiss him—and quiet him. Too many questions were never a good thing, and Luc's purpose on this journey wasn't to be her interrogator. He glared at her with mock ferocity before kissing her back.

"My family was whole once, before they came to Virginia," Rebekah mused, linking her arm through his and resuming their stroll toward the first houses of the little village. The sun wouldn't rise for at least another hour. "But a plague took my oldest sister, and after she died my father wanted to take us to a place where we'd be safe. I was born in the New World, not far from here. My parents thought they had saved us."

Luc glanced at her. "There are plenty of other dangers here," he pointed out.

"Exactly." One of the horses whickered softly behind them, and Rebekah scanned the dark trees that surrounded them. "Our small village neighbored a werewolf clan, and I lost another brother to their violence. My parents realized then that nowhere was truly safe. They could run forever, but they would keep losing children everywhere they went."

"And yet here you are today," Luc reminded her. "Whole and living and, if I may say so, in *extremely* good health."

Rebekah smiled ruefully, unable to deny it. In his usual, direct way, Luc had struck on the same logic that had motivated her mother to change her children into vampires. Esther had believed—at the time, at least— that strength and life were all that mattered, even if they cost her family everything else.

"My mother was a witch," Rebekah explained. "She was an exceptionally powerful one, and she cast an immortality curse on us—"

"I've heard you call it a curse before," Luc interrupted. "But I don't understand why you use that word for a never-ending life."

"It's a *curse*." Her voice was forceful, but she knew Luc was too newly made to understand. She saw Marguerite's glassy brown eyes, her auburn hair spread out like a fan across Rebekah's pillows. Leaving her there had been an extra little twist of the dagger from Klaus, a reminder that nothing was safe from his reach. The cruelty he had once reserved for his enemies had been directed squarely at her, the sister who had promised to stand by him forever.

"I was there when the spell was cast. My mother made us as strong as she knew how to, but the price of that strength was terrible. The hunger—you've felt that, and you know how it tears at us. She imagined us running through the hills, free again from fear, but every touch of the sun scorched our skin. We were confined to the night, and our neighbors grew distrustful of our new, strange habits. Soon they wanted nothing to do with us, and we quickly learned that it was within their power to bar us from their homes. We couldn't enter without their invitation, and no one was willing to offer it."

"People fear what they don't know." Luc shrugged, as if the total isolation faced by the Mikaelsons were just some trivial faux pas. "But the benefits, surely, outweighed those minor concerns."

"Our mother thought so at first," Rebekah admitted. "She thought that our safety was worth any price, until she saw the life she had condemned us to. She regretted her choice, and my father went even further than that. He vowed to use his own immortality to destroy ours, to kill the children he had once demanded that his wife save."

"But you cannot be killed." Luc frowned. The serious expression suited his handsome face: all squared angles and broad planes.

The Originals certainly didn't go spreading rumors about their mortal flaw, but all strengths came with a weakness. Their mother had called upon the power of the White Oak tree to grant her children immortality, and the wood of that same tree could take it away again. The siblings had burned the tree to the ground, but Rebekah had heard whispers that it stood again in Mystic Falls, every bit as immortal as the Mikaelsons were. She had chosen Luc to escort her there, to learn if those rumors were true, but even now she was reluctant to explain the Mikaelsons' greatest weakness to him.

"Every curse is complicated, as is my family," she compromised.

"Then it's just as well to have some time away from them," he said mischievously. Luc was a straightforward man with simple tastes—the intrigue of the Originals must have seemed impossibly foreign to him.

Between thoughts of her past and thoughts of Luc, Rebekah was so distracted that she was startled to realize they had reached the outskirts of the village. A small inn lay at the end of a dirt road. When they knocked on the thick wooden door, a bleary-eyed woman peered out of a small window, suspicious of the couple arriving on her doorstep before the sky was even light.

"Our horses need tending," Rebekah announced. The door didn't budge. "I can pay in silver," Rebekah went on. She jingled a pouch of coins in her palm, letting the weight of the silver be heard.

The door creaked open, "Why didn't you say so?" the woman replied. "Come in, please, madame. And monsieur."

Luc followed a groom to the stables, and Rebekah noticed that he trailed the man at a bit of a distance, keeping out of his line of sight. "We'll need a room just for the day," she said to the woman, curious what Luc was up to. With a last glance back at him, Rebekah stepped inside the inn.

The innkeeper fished around for a room key, still eyeing Rebekah doubtfully. "These parts aren't always safe at night," she ventured. "It's lucky you and your husband made it here unharmed. Wouldn't you rather stay over until the next morning to travel on by day? There's a lovely room with a view over the valley, much nicer for a young couple like yourselves than those treacherous roads after dark."

"Consider it, darling." Luc appeared again at her elbow, looking unnaturally flushed. Rebekah thought she could spot a tiny fleck of blood in the corner of his mouth. "I would hate to risk our safety, no matter how much of a hurry you're in."

She looked up at him, trying to read his bland, polite smile. His thick blond hair was tied back away from his face with a strip of leather, and she was struck by a sudden impulse to let it down and run her fingers through it. "Let us see the room," she agreed. "It might be nice to rest awhile."

Seemingly reassured, the innkeeper turned toward the wooden staircase. Luc fell on her as soon as her back was turned, wrapping a hand around her mouth and sinking his teeth into her neck. His skin still looked tanned against the woman's sallow flesh, even though it had been weeks since he had seen the sun.

He punctured the innkeeper's jugular vein and then passed her to Rebekah, his blue eyes glittering eagerly. She needed no more urging than that: She drank deeply, savoring the feel of the woman's fluttering heart. Her kind had been made to hunt humans, not for all of this backstabbing and infighting. This was what the Mikaelsons should have been doing all along, rather than scheming and maneuvering and betraying one another. Klaus had lost touch with his own nature, and for a while he had managed to drag Rebekah into the darkness with him.

"I thought you could use a bit of a diversion," Luc

suggested when the woman fell to the floor. "Perhaps an inn full of distractions will take your mind from the troubles that have driven you from New Orleans."

There was a noise on the staircase: a patron with the bad judgment to be an early riser. Rebekah smiled and positioned herself out of sight, lying in wait as the man descended the stairs. She could have rushed at him, but Luc was right: After the night she'd had, a little fun was in order. Playing with her food was always enjoyable, and Rebekah found herself growing excited at the thought of picking off the guests one by one.

By noon the body count included all the visitors of the inn, as well as the keeper's husband, a milkman, and an exceptionally pretty young chambermaid. Rebekah felt nearly drunk on all the blood she had consumed, and its heat radiated out from her skin.

She slipped out of her dusty traveling gown and then the shift she wore beneath it, letting her golden hair down for good measure. She could feel every tiny movement in the currents of the air, she could hear earthworms pushing through the dirt two floors beneath her bare feet. She felt almost human again . . . only better.

The bedroom where they had ended their merry hunt was by far the best of the lot, although the windows were carefully shuttered against the view. But even in the semidarkness, Rebekah could feel the heat of the sun overhead as if its light were streaming out through her own skin. She raised her arms and Luc stepped into them, his lips crushing down on hers with even more passion than usual.

Rebekah helped him out of his clothes, not caring that his tunic landed on an ice-cold, bloodless corpse. They barely made it to the four-poster bed before their bodies came together, moving as one to the beat of their racing pulses. Luc invented a hundred new ways to worship her, reminding her over and over again of the urgency of his desire for her. Rebekah spent hours learning the sensual curve of his lips, the touch of his calloused hands, the feel of the sharp ridges of his hip bones against her own.

She had chosen well indeed. He was exactly the man to fill the idle hours between here and Mystic Falls.

THREE

*E*lijah was not a man who hid in darkness. By his very nature he struck fear into others. He didn't need to think about commonplace dangers, especially not in the city he had called his own for so long. New Orleans had been his home for the better part of a century, and yet tonight he found himself hiding in the shadows of a narrow alleyway like a criminal.

Elijah had suspected for some time that Klaus was up to no good. It had started with his brother moving out of the family mansion—proof enough that he was hatching some troublesome plot. And then the new vampires had appeared in the streets. Overnight, there were more of them than they'd made in the last twenty years, and there was only one plausible explanation: Klaus was raising an army, and havoc was sure to follow.

On the street corner, a vampire accosted a prostitute, and Elijah forced himself to do nothing. It would likely be her last night alive, but Elijah couldn't afford to be caught—or have his whereabouts reported to Klaus. By the next night the girl would either be dead or a vampire herself. Elijah waited until the pair was engaged to the point of distraction, then moved on.

It was the second time tonight that Elijah had been forced to sneak through the shadows. Earlier, he'd been forced to slip out of the mansion without getting caught by Lisette. His former lover seemed to be everywhere, waiting around every corner and behind every door like a lovely, flame-haired punishment. She had every right to her anger, but Elijah wasn't prepared to bear the brunt of it every time he stepped out of his bedroom or study, and so he avoided her.

Elijah had adored Lisette, and his time with her had restored more of his faith in the world than he'd realized he'd lost. But the Mikaelsons had enemies everywhere, including some exceptionally dangerous ones within their own family. Ultimately, their romance had simply been too public.

No matter how brash or capable she was, Lisette could never be more than a second-generation vampire.

She was a hair slower and a shade weaker than Klaus and Rebekah, and worst of all she could be killed by a simple wooden stake through the heart.

His love for her made Elijah vulnerable. Any danger to Lisette was a threat to him, and her own bravery, which bordered on recklessness, didn't help matters. She refused to be careful, and she accused him of wanting to keep her locked up and away from the world.

She wasn't wrong, but Elijah felt like his hands were tied. And when Klaus had threatened to decapitate her—for the hundredth time—over some minor dispute about using a werewolf-owned vendor at his precious whorehouse, Elijah had finally understood that he had no choice. Klaus had grown increasingly volatile, and more than one head had already rolled before his wrath. The next could be hers.

And yet Elijah knew Lisette would never forgive him for his weakness in ending their relationship, no matter how pure his intentions had been. It was easier to avoid her than to face the constant, silent accusation on her face, the reminder that he had given her up in order not to lose her.

Elijah had spotted her just outside the front door of the mansion that very night. At least she only put herself in his way—she had far too much pride to follow him. Elijah wondered what she would do if she happened to stumble across one of his meetings with Alejandra. Would knowledge of his new lover free Lisette from her need to haunt him? Or would it make her want to burn down his house—perhaps with him still inside it?

A pair of vampires burst out of a tavern in front of him. Elijah darted sideways into the slim cover of a doorway. That wouldn't have been enough to keep a more experienced hunter's eyes off him, but these two were newly made, and drunk on both blood and ale. Elijah held every muscle in his body perfectly still until they had passed, their raucous singing echoing off the cobblestoned street.

When the way was clear, Elijah moved on, all his senses alert, anticipating his first glimpse of the woman he would soon hold in his arms.

He had first met Alejandra Vargas at the Southern Spot, of all places, when he had gone to warn his brother that his raids on werewolf holdings weren't as discreet as Klaus believed them to be. The wolves were starting to retaliate, disrupting the imports and exports that Elijah had delegated to Klaus, and at this rate it wouldn't be long before war broke out once again. Elijah had been prepared to bully Klaus back into line, but the sight of the brothel's new fortune-teller had knocked the fight right out of his body.

He could tell at a glance that Alejandra wasn't one of

the establishment's usual women. She was tall—nearly as tall as he was—with curling black hair and startling green eyes that seemed to pin him to the door the moment he walked through it. The purring accent Elijah heard when she spoke was full of intelligence, mystery, and humor, and he was enchanted at once.

"Please sit," she had told him, an order masquerading as a request.

Elijah had suspected that Klaus was in one of the back rooms with two or three of his more buxom employees. Ever since he'd won the brothel back for the fourth time, Klaus had seemed dedicated to enjoying his ownership to the fullest, and Elijah had decided that his business with his brother could wait. He had sat in the chair Alejandra indicated, and she settled herself across from him. Women moved in and out of the main room, mingling with customers and occasionally peeling off to more private areas, but Elijah only had eyes for the fortune-teller.

"You have interesting hands," she had informed him, brushing one fingertip along the lines that cut across his palm.

"I might say the same," he replied. Her fingers were decorated with precious stones set into heavy, intricate rings. Each of them must have cost more than she could make in a year reading palms, and he wondered what had prompted her to seek out such work. He doubted that she needed whatever Klaus's clientele was willing to pay.

"Then perhaps you should tell me *my* future," she teased, catching his wrist more firmly and holding his palm toward the light of the nearest candle.

"You can't read your own?" Elijah asked, twisting his hand so that he could study hers more closely. Her skin was warm and supple. "What kind of a gift is that?"

"I'm not so arrogant as to want to know my own future," Alejandra said, "so whatever you see you may keep to yourself. But you, señor, have pride to spare. I can see it here"—she touched the base of his thumb, sending thrills up his entire arm—"and here, as well." Her fingernail rested in a second spot on his palm, and he stared at it, fascinated.

"You may have me confused with my brother," Elijah murmured. "I simply prefer to be prepared for whatever might come my way."

"Your brother?" Alejandra asked, adjusting the angle of his hand again. "You have more than just the one. Your family is closer-knit than most."

Elijah chuckled at the understatement. "We can't seem to escape one another," he confirmed. Even Kol and Finn, staked by Klaus centuries before, had remained with their siblings. They slept deeply in coffins that the Originals had carried back and forth across the world. "Family is forever."

Alejandra smiled as if he had reminded her of some private joke between them, as if they were old friends who knew each other's secrets. To his surprise, Elijah had to actually remind himself to be cautious. She was a stranger, however appealing she might be.

"I hope you like them, then," she told him, her voice brimming with laughter. "This line here is your life line, and it is . . . *exceptionally* long."

The words might have been innocent enough: Surely it was good for business to assure her customers of long and healthy lives. But there was no doubt in Elijah's mind that Alejandra had known exactly what he really was, and that she had known it before he'd walked through the door.

It was true that the supernatural inhabitants of New Orleans had grown overconfident, perhaps even careless. Rumors of their existence had become an open secret in the past few decades. Ordinary citizens knew what sort of creatures lived in their midst, and Elijah had been surprised to discover how much Alejandra knew about his kind and their rivals—more than any human should have, really.

He had been thoroughly charmed, but forced himself to proceed cautiously. The last woman Elijah had found so intriguing had been used against him. Lisette was lost to him because he had pursued a life with her too eagerly.

There was a stirring in the darkness in front of him, and Elijah tensed, ready to fight. But it was Alejandra who stepped out into the starlight, her body swathed in a hooded black cloak. She had kept up her work at the Southern Spot to avoid raising Klaus's suspicions, and she smelled of smoke, whiskey, and lust.

Beneath the hood he could just make out her sharp, strong chin, her high forehead, and the midnight curls of her hair. Elijah longed to push the hood back and kiss her, but he could hear more than one set of footsteps nearby and he couldn't risk being caught with her in the open.

He wrapped an arm around her instead, guiding her wordlessly toward the house he had prepared for their rendezvous. The previous occupant had been a politician who leaned a bit too far toward the werewolves' interests for Elijah's taste, so his death had served a variety of purposes all at once. "Here," he said, opening the door and then stepping back to let Alejandra enter first.

He caught her in the hallway, spinning her back into his arms before the door had fully closed behind him, and kissing her deep red lips.

FOUR

Klaus's eyes scanned the torchlit streets of the Werewolves' quarter. There was no sign of movement, no hint of a watch being kept. Were they *that* secure in their power? The werewolves were all sleeping, confident in their plan to attack his vampires in the morning. Guillaume had confirmed it on the hour—he'd spied the pack leader, Sampson Collado, going over his final strategy that afternoon. But Klaus would have the upper hand this night, just the way he had intended it.

"Drive them out of their homes," he reminded his soldiers. They were new to their strength, new to their heightened reflexes, senses, and appetites. A little practice would do them good, and what better training than a raid on the actual enemy? "Aggravate them, disrupt them. Don't get pinned down; just turn the quarter inside out and then regroup at the garrison."

Klaus heard an appreciative rumble spread through his army. They were eager for a fight, eager to impress the more experienced vampires and especially their invincible general. This sort of raid was more than just a drill: It would help to separate the wheat from the chaff.

"It's not too late to reconsider," a voice beside Klaus's ear warned, and he gritted his teeth together before turning to stare down its owner. *Oh, Lisette.* Lisette had been pleasant enough before she had taken up with Elijah, but over the years her loyalty to her lover had grown increasingly irritating. Now that Elijah had ended their romance and taken up with some two-bit whorehouse fortune-teller, the fact that Lisette still took his brother's side over Klaus's was almost infuriating. "We could stick to their storehouses and shops, to disrupt them without showing our hand. There's no need to provoke open war."

Her gray eyes were so earnest that Klaus could almost believe she was speaking for herself, rather than just parroting his brother's usual ideas. *Don't make trouble, don't strike first, better to be the victim than the aggressor.* . . . Klaus didn't know how Elijah could stand it. The Mikaelsons' lives were far too long to waste responding and reacting and hesitating century after century. They were entitled to forge their own fates.

"There's no *need*," he agreed icily. "If you'd rather sit at home, Lisette, and wait for the wolves to come to your door, you're welcome to do so. But if that's the case, then it's a toss up over who will kill you first—me or them."

She tossed her red-blonde hair back over her shoulder, the expression on her freckled face stopping just short of outright defiance. They had been friendly once, but Klaus knew better than to trust her now. Lisette's association with Elijah had tainted her, and if she intended to prove herself in Klaus's army, then she was already off to a bad start, talented warrior or not.

"I'll take a group around to the south," she informed him, her voice clipped and nearly as cold as his own. "We can keep an eye on the perimeter for you."

"You want to watch my back?" He let his face convey the depth of his skepticism, but he signaled to a nearby cluster of vampires and gestured for them to follow Lisette. "Fine, then," he said. "Show me how committed you are to our cause, Lisette. I'll be watching with great interest."

She stalked off without another word, and about a dozen vampires followed her. Klaus looked back over his army, crammed into the narrow streets of the Werewolves' quarter like a deadly wave about to break.

"Go," he commanded, and they leapt forward as one, pouring along the cobblestones toward the dark houses where their enemies slept.

Klaus heard the crash of a door falling inward, then another, and the first shrill screams pierced the cool night air. The werewolves were stronger than humans, but without a full moon to unleash their true strength, his vampires easily overwhelmed them.

A woman ran out into the street in a thin gray nightgown, clutching handfuls of jewelry to her chest while the telltale sounds of ransacking drifted out from the house behind her. Klaus intercepted her smoothly, blocking her path before she even had time to realize she wasn't alone in the street. "Allow me to take those for you, madame," he suggested, taking the treasure from her unresisting hands. "I wouldn't want them to weigh you down while you run." His fangs snapped into full view, and the woman took the hint and ran for her life.

The sounds of fighting filled the quarter, rising from every house and alley. Klaus prowled along the dark streets, monitoring the progress of his soldiers. By his count he had lost two already, dead so quickly that he was confident they wouldn't be missed. Lisette's group was nowhere to be seen, and he refused to hunt for them. If she really was patrolling the edges of the quarter, he would see evidence of it sooner or later.

If she wasn't, Klaus would chase her down and leave her corpse for Elijah to discover.

"This way!" came a whispering hiss from his left, and Klaus's senses adjusted to the soft footfalls behind him. He counted three of them: young male werewolves who had formed their own little resistance on the spot.

Klaus smiled to himself and stood perfectly still, waiting for them to get close. He couldn't tell if they recognized him or not, but it was obvious that they had no idea what he was capable of. He felt their breath on the back of his neck just before two of them grabbed him by the arms, and then, at last, he moved.

Klaus wrenched his shoulders into motion and forced his hands toward each other, smashing the wolves' heads together with a sickening crack. The third one threw an arm around Klaus's neck, trying to strangle him or just hold on, but Klaus flipped him forward onto the cobblestones and then kicked him viciously in his side. The young man coughed and spat up blood, but one of the first two attackers staggered back up to his feet.

"I didn't come to kill tonight," Klaus told him, relaxing into a ready stance. "There's no reason you can't still walk away."

The werewolf hesitated, glancing down at his two fallen friends, then back along the empty street as if he hoped to see reinforcements. A scream rose from a nearby house, before cutting off abruptly. "You attacked us in our beds, monster," the werewolf reminded Klaus through gritted teeth. "If you didn't come to kill, then I hope you came prepared to die."

He took a powerful jump off the ground, leaping through the air so forcefully that he could have been in his wolf form. But when his blow landed, Klaus could feel just how badly his strength fell short. He was more than an ordinary human, perhaps, but he wasn't even close to a match for a Mikaelson.

Klaus caught the werewolf's arm and snapped it like a reed, and the young man howled in pain. But he lashed out with his good arm, ready to fight to the last, and in spite of himself Klaus had to admire that in an opponent. "I told you I didn't come to kill *tonight*," he repeated, parrying the blow and throwing the youth against a timbered wall. "But I'll be back another night. It's your choice whether you want to live for now."

The werewolf dropped into a crouch, winded from the impact, but struggling not to show weakness. His deep-set eyes glowed yellow out of a thin, clever face, and his shoulders were wiry and strong. He had been bred to attack Klaus's kind on sight, but he seemed to have a bit of common sense floating around in his instinct-addled brain as well.

The werewolf looked around, registering the sounds of violence and fear that were everywhere. Klaus waited for the young wolf to realize there was nothing to be gained by dying in an empty alleyway.

"I won't forget this, vampire," the young man said at last, as ominously as he could manage under the circumstances. A faint gurgling sound came from the unconscious wolf whose ribs Klaus had cracked, while the other lay motionless.

"You'll remember that I let you live?" Klaus asked, raising one eyebrow in mock surprise. "Gratitude isn't what your kind is known for, but I suppose there are exceptions to every rule."

The werewolf snarled, his eyes burning an even deeper yellow, but he was beaten and he knew it. He turned and fled, disappearing down the twisting streets and back into the chaos of the Werewolves' quarter.

Klaus caught just the faintest whiff of smoke as he watched the youth go, and he wondered if his soldiers were getting carried away. Enthusiasm was important, but Klaus had no use for loose cannons. He followed the scent, ready to deal with whichever vampires had gone rogue. The city was Klaus's prize, the compensation—

however inadequate—for all that had been taken from him.

If anyone was going to burn it to the ground, it would be him.

"You there!" he called when he saw a few vampires hurrying out of a house like thieves in the night. It was the next house down that was burning; he could see the sinister flickering of flames through the shutters. "Were you in that home just now?"

One of them glanced over his shoulder at the house, and Klaus thought he detected some guilt in the man's eyes. He snapped the vampire's neck without another word.

"I thought I was clear," he snarled at the others, who shrank away from him in fear. "The werewolves aren't such a formidable threat that we need to smoke them out. I intend to own this quarter, and so anyone who damages it risks making himself my enemy. I suggest a bit more caution—because the next time this happens you might as well do yourself a favor and burn with it."

He stalked away, listening to the whimper of the fallen vampire as his spine began to snap itself back into place. Just then, Lisette emerged from the burning house.

"It's out," she said when she reached him. "You should tell your people to be more careful."

"I thought you were one of 'my people,'" he reminded her, a sharp, warning note in his voice.

"Of course." She flipped her red-gold hair behind her shoulders and crossed her arms over her chest. "That's why I'm here, putting out your fires. Watching your back, just like I said I would."

He stepped closer to her, watching for any sign that she might flinch. "You *said* you'd patrol the perimeter," he pointed out. "The edge of the quarter is blocks away from here, and yet here you are."

A werewolf family ran along the street, each of them carrying a bundle of their belongings on their backs. Klaus watched them flee with disinterest—it was the wolves who'd held their ground and defended their homes who would pose a challenge the next time around.

"Lucky for you I returned," she answered gamely. "I smelled the smoke and I came. Look how high the moon has gotten. Half of your soldiers are already making their way back to the garrison, and the ones who chose to linger did so at their own risk. The raid was over."

Klaus wanted to shake her until her fangs rattled, to knock some fear into her stubborn head. One wrong word, one obviously false note, and he would kill her and be done with it. Klaus might just have to force her hand, was all.

"Join them at the garrison," he ordered, his mind made up. "Join them and start coordinating with the group leaders who have made it back. You'll be planning our next attack, love, and you will be leading the charge."

FIVE

*T*he closer they rode to Mystic Falls, the more Rebekah felt like there was a strange buzzing in her bones. She could almost hear it, the trembling anticipation of her homecoming.

Rebekah hadn't been to Mystic Falls in nearly a thousand years, but she could still picture how it had looked on the night she left. She hadn't aged a day since then, but those centuries must have reshaped her former home. Even though she looked the same, Rebekah was a different person, changed in countless other ways.

As Luc lead the way, pressing northward through the lush Virginia forests, all Rebekah could see was the countryside she had once known. She had run through these trees; she had dreamed beneath their shade. Even the smell of the air was familiar: rich dirt and the beginnings of spring.

"We are close—I remember the tree being not far from here," Luc said, pulling a compass from his pocket. Starlight gleamed in his blue eyes as he turned to look at her. "You seem as though you belong here. Do you know the rest of the way?"

"Almost," Rebekah said in a soft voice. She could feel the humming inside her, the thrill of being back at the source of her power. At any moment, she knew she would recognize a path or the fork of a tree, and she would be back. She could almost hear her brothers' voices and feel the play of dappled sunlight on her skin.

"Is anyone expecting us?" Luc asked lightly. Rebekah couldn't imagine being so casual or incurious, but Luc's straightforward mind was part of his charm.

"I don't think anyone would be happy to see a Mikaelson returning to this land," Rebekah sighed. It may have been generations since Mystic Falls had laid eyes on an Original vampire, but Rebekah was sure that they would recognize her on sight. Fortunately, making friends wasn't the goal of this journey. All she needed was the White Oak tree, or whatever remained of it.

The trees began to thin, and Rebekah could make out the roll of fields below the black sky full of stars.

"Not far now," she told Luc, hearing the strain in her voice. "Keep back from the tree line."

"Oh, is our presence here a secret?" Luc asked teasingly. "I didn't realize there was something you were keeping to yourself."

In spite of her tension, Rebekah laughed. "You've been more than patient," she admitted. "But consider carefully, Luc. You know who I am and what sort of problems tend to find me. If there's something I haven't told you, are you sure that you want to hear it? It's not especially safe to be in the inner circle of my family."

Shadows of bare branches broke up the faint starlight that fell on his face, and Rebekah couldn't be sure she was reading his expression properly. Luc looked almost hungry, so desperate to know her secrets that for a moment she thought she could see his fangs. It was so unlike him, so opposite of everything she had come to appreciate about his relaxed charm, that Rebekah felt herself shudder in unwelcome surprise.

But when she looked again, turning her head to see him more clearly, she could find no trace of that eagerness. She wondered if the magic that still lingered here might be playing tricks on her. Mystic Falls was too layered with pain and desire for Rebekah to trust her instincts, and the odd buzzing felt like someone was sawing at her bones.

"It's just a tree you need. How special could it be?" Luc said.

"More than you would ever believe," Rebekah said, rising up in her stirrups to catch her first glimpse of the roofs of Mystic Falls. "We're going to use this tree to kill one of my brothers."

The White Oak came into sight, standing proudly in the center of an open field, just as it had been when Esther had first performed the immortality spell. Just as it had been before Rebekah and her siblings had burned it to the ground. She had known in her heart that the tree would survive somehow, but seeing it there, so exactly the same in every detail, was disorienting. It was as if she had been dragged backward in time, as if centuries of life were nothing but a long, painful dream.

Rebekah dismounted and walked toward the tree. "Don't you have a hundred more questions now than you did before?" she asked, letting her words drift back over her shoulder. "Don't you even want to know which of my brothers I intend to kill?"

Before Luc could answer, a shadow at the base of the tree shifted and stretched. Rebekah immediately felt all her muscles tense, and from his silence she knew that Luc had seen it, too.

"That's an easy question," a voice drawled, and a man stepped out from between the tree's gnarled roots, coming into the starlight. "Naturally you plan to kill Niklaus."

"And should I find out who you are before I kill *you*?" Rebekah put the full force of compulsion into her words. The man was dressed all in black, with leather boots that came up over the knees of his breeches. A silver pin glinted softly at the throat of his full cloak. He was tall and slender with black hair that curled to his shoulders and dark olive skin. Rebekah knew at once that she had never seen him before, but he seemed to know her.

"My name is Tomás," he responded. His tone was courteous and pleasant, but Rebekah sensed that he was answering of his own free will, not in response to any power of hers. His mind was immune to her control, and in her experience that never meant anything but trouble. "I've been waiting for you."

"If I'd known that," Rebekah murmured, scanning his face for some clue to his intentions, "I might have ridden faster."

"You might not have," Tomás countered, as amiably as if they were old friends. "But fast or slow, I knew you would come."

"Explain yourself," she said. She'd thought she might be recognized in Mystic Falls, but she could hear the sound of the bayou in Tomás's voice. He didn't belong here, and there was no way he could have known she was coming. She hadn't even know it herself until Marguerite had been killed.

"I'm not here to answer your questions," he chided, and she felt her fangs click out. His voice felt like cold fingers creeping along her spine, and his eyes might have been chips of green ice. "I'm here, Rebekah Mikaelson, because I will be your death."

He meant it—there wasn't even the faintest shadow of doubt in her mind. He had the ease and confidence of a man who expected to succeed. For a human to seek out two vampires in the middle of the night meant he was sure of his own invincibility.

"Kill him," Rebekah ordered through gritted teeth, and Luc leapt forward to obey.

He was fast, but Tomás was faster. His right hand flicked outward, casting a fine spray of shimmering powder into Luc's snarling face. The vampire howled in pain and crashed to his knees. Rebekah ran to him. Luc writhed and scratched at his eyes, and she held his wrists tightly, trying to contain him, but his brute strength and desperation made it almost impossible.

"What did you do to him?" Rebekah demanded.

"This is only the beginning," Tomás told her, his tone still light. "And tonight I'm only the messenger. You're going to lose everything that you love, Rebekah, and then you will lose your life."

He strolled into the night, keeping his back to Rebekah with such casual arrogance that she felt frozen in place. She held Luc's body pinned against her own, as if by keeping him close she could protect him from whatever Tomás's powder had done to him.

As she rocked Luc against her chest, her mind raced. Who was Tomás? And where could a mere human find the power to take down a vampire? It was a mystery that suddenly required all her attention.

She wasn't about to lose anyone else; not that night. First Klaus had lost his last shred of decency, costing Rebekah her dearest friend and any hope she'd once had for her brother in one vicious stroke. And now there was another madman on the loose, who endangered even more of the people in Rebekah's life. Klaus's meeting with a White Oak stake would have to wait.

No one threatened Rebekah Mikaelson and got away with it.

SIX

$\mathcal{E}$ lijah awoke with a sudden, disorienting jolt. None of his surroundings were familiar, and he blinked for a moment at the strange furniture and wrong light. From outside came screams, howls, and the grinding crunch of metal against stone—the sounds of battle, which hardly narrowed things down for a man like Elijah. Then he felt the warmth of a woman by his side and he remembered where he was. But why was there violence in the Werewolves' quarter when they were so far from the full moon?

Alejandra stirred a bit, then rolled, exposing her lovely naked body to the starlight that streamed in through the windows. She slept like she didn't have a care in the world, and Elijah planted a kiss between her breasts, wishing he could manage such a peaceful rest.

Another scream came from outside the house, and the light that danced across Alejandra's skin had the yellow-red glow of fire. Elijah bolted upright, warning Alejandra to stay where she was with one outstretched hand. *"Shh,"* he whispered.

Elijah had assumed that Klaus would avoid this part of town, but from the sound of it, Elijah had underestimated his brother's common sense. Klaus's vampires were charging through the streets to the south, and Elijah found himself on the edge of a war zone.

"Is that what I think it is?" Alejandra asked, her voice low and soft. "I had heard rumors—" She hesitated, biting her lower lip. "You seemed so sure the peace would hold that I ignored them."

"It seems I was mistaken," Elijah muttered, pulling on his clothes without lighting any lamps. Truce or no truce, he should have known that Klaus would find a way to ruin a perfectly enjoyable night. "You should be safe here until dawn if you don't do anything to draw their attention."

"Then you do believe it's Klaus?" Alejandra asked, relaxing back into the tangled sheets with a meaningful sigh. Elijah could see a crease of disapproval between her eyebrows, and he deliberately looked away. "You would stay if it were anyone but Klaus. My darling, you can't spend your entire life chasing after him."

Elijah had certainly heard that argument before over the centuries—frequently from his own mouth. But it was his duty to stop Klaus when he began to stray down some new, dangerous path. They were family, and whatever his brother did was Elijah's concern, whether he wanted that burden or not.

The flames in the house across the way began to subside, and Elijah could swear he heard his brother's voice outside—and possibly…Lisette's? Had she finally abandoned him and teamed up with his brother? He didn't dare look out the window to find out.

At least his brother wasn't committed to burning New Orleans to the ground. He was *just* undoing a full generation of diplomacy with one ill-conceived midnight raid.

"I don't have the luxury of ignoring him," Elijah said, jamming one foot into its boot, then the other. He caught a glimpse of his face in the gilt-framed mirror on the far wall and looked away. "My family is a complicated matter, Alejandra. You know I would rather be here with you than out there cleaning up after Niklaus, but—"

"Don't lie for my benefit, Elijah. I knew what I was

getting into with you," she said, her voice low but hard. She sat up, holding the sheets against her bare chest. "Your siblings dictate our entire relationship. Sneaking around so that they don't find out, you always running off to deal with one of them . . . It's as if you think them incapable of navigating the world without you. They're powerful, nearly invincible creatures with centuries of experience to guide them. You have a choice in how you devote your energy, and I see the way you choose."

Elijah felt his jaw clench. Even after all the precautions he had taken to keep this part of his life separate from the rest, Klaus still managed to intrude. "You've never had siblings, my love," he began again, trying to sound more patient than he felt. None of this mess was Alejandra's fault, after all. "We made a vow to remain together, to take care of each other throughout eternity. I never expected that to be easy, but it *has* also been our greatest strength. We need each other, even if sometimes we may wish we didn't."

"So Klaus *needs* you now?" Alejandra tossed the sheet aside in disgust and reached for her shift where it lay crumpled beside the bed. Her skin gleamed like fresh cream, and Elijah watched the curve of her back as she bent over. "I'm sure he would be pleased if you held his coat for him while he razed the Werewolves' quarter to the ground."

"He needs me to stop him," Elijah growled. Klaus certainly wasn't going to stop on his own—self-control was simply not a part of his character. "Niklaus always had it harder than the rest of us, even before we learned that our father wasn't his. All the ugliness of *that* discovery has haunted him his entire life. He needs more watching, and sometimes more patience, than you would expect. There's history here, Alejandra, that you can't possibly understand."

"I understand better than you think I do," she countered, rising to her bare feet. The floorboards creaked a little beneath her weight, although the sound was muffled by a rich Oriental carpet. Alejandra's hair curled around her like a dark halo, catching every glimmer from the light outside. "My work is about the future, and you can't build a future by living in the past—even your siblings have realized that. Niklaus is no longer some wounded boy rebelling against his stepfather's resentment. Rebekah isn't that hopeful dreamer of a girl you always seem to describe. You say it's about history, but history didn't end the night you died. You have all continued to grow and change every night for centuries . . . or at least, *they* have."

"Rebekah was the first of us to say we should stay together," Elijah argued, his stubbornness getting the better of him. He didn't want to fight with Alejandra. "She would agree with me that family comes first."

"And imagine how much happier she would be if she didn't," Alejandra urged, resting a hand on his forearm. The last time she had touched him like that was only an hour ago—they'd been making love, and she'd pinned him down—but it felt almost like a lifetime. "Your sister has been trying to break free of that promise for centuries, and your brother has never even bothered to honor it. I know how much of yourself you have devoted to your family, darling, but when have they ever shown you the same kind of respect? Why does the burden always fall on you?"

"Because I can shoulder it." Elijah frowned at the naïveté of the question. There was a shout and then the ring of broken glass. "When something is necessary and I am capable, should I sit back and complain that no one else is doing it? Would that be the attitude of a man you could respect?"

"'When something is necessary,'" Alejandra repeated, her voice a low thrum in the quiet of the room. "Of course I would always wish you to do what is *necessary*."

He stepped away from her, needing some physical distance between them in order to think properly. The sight and smell of her was intoxicating. When she stood so close, in only that thin linen shift, it was almost impossible to collect his wits enough to argue with her. If she were a witch, Elijah would have sworn she had cast some kind of spell on him, but Alejandra Vargas was human through and through.

"I've been alive a lot longer than you," Elijah said after a pause, knowing that it was a position of last resort. "I think I have a better perspective on what needs to be done."

"Or perhaps you could benefit from a fresh pair of eyes," Alejandra suggested, her own glittering like emeralds in the faint light. "The world has changed, my love. New Orleans has changed, and humans have changed, and so have your siblings. The only thing that hasn't changed in all that long life of yours is you."

Elijah bristled at the accusation, but there was a splinter of truth in her stake.

"I am the foundation of my family," he said, more to himself than to Alejandra. "I am what they need me to be." Without Elijah, Klaus and Rebekah would have been adrift, lost inside their own immortality. Kol and Finn would be buried somewhere and forgotten. Without Elijah, everything would have fallen apart over and over again until there was nothing left.

"What about what you need?" Alejandra purred, closing the distance between them. The smell of smoke lingered in her hair, left over from her evening of work at the Southern Spot. It made him feel a little dizzy, but he inhaled even more deeply all the same. "What can I give you?" She wrapped her arms around his waist, brushing her chest against his.

She looked for a moment as though she wanted to say more, her teeth closing uncertainly on her bottom lip.

"This isn't about me," Elijah assured her, bringing his hands down to her hips and drawing her closer. "Niklaus's conflict with the werewolves goes back far longer than the Collados. He can't help but hate them, but I can get him to stand down."

"But if everything I've heard is now coming true . . ." She trailed off and laid her head against his shoulder, looking out the window. "Well. As you say, you've known your brother longer than anyone."

Alejandra stepped away from him, retrieving her gown from the back of a chair. She seemed preoccupied, and her sudden withdrawal struck Elijah like a physical blow. He certainly hadn't taken any pleasure in arguing with her, but it was almost painful to be dismissed so abruptly.

"Tell me what you've heard," he urged, reaching out to take hold of her arm, to stop her from leaving. "I want to know."

Alejandra's eyes flickered to the window again, and then back to Elijah's. "I don't really understand it myself," she admitted, "especially in light of tonight's raid. But there were some unusual guests at the Southern Spot this evening, and some bits of conversation, rumors have been floating around all week. . . . I don't have any proof, my darling, and I don't want to be the messenger for ugly gossip."

"There can be truth in gossip," Elijah countered, "or it can point the way to the truth. I would rather you tell me everything, and I can decide what to believe."

Alejandra let her gown fall back to the floorboards in a pile of soft, mysterious folds, and showed him her open palms as if in surrender. "What I've heard, Elijah, is that your brother is working *with* the wolves rather than against them. That he has a pact with Sampson Collado, and that the escalating tension between them has been nothing but a ruse."

"A ruse to what end?" Elijah asked, shocked to hear such a dangerous strategy. "What could those two stand to gain from pretending to be enemies? Alejandra, such an alliance would never happen."

"Common foes make for unlikely friends," she whispered, biting at her soft lower lip again.

"There's no one they hate more than each other, is there?" He let the question hang in the air.

But perhaps there *was* one thing that could unite Klaus and werewolves, one man who could align his brother with the detested Collados.

"There is you," Alejandra said, and in his heart Elijah knew she was right.

SEVEN

*K*laus tipped another glass of whiskey into his mouth, setting off roars of approval from his new friends. The raid had gone even better than he had hoped, especially considering how green his soldiers had been at the outset. There had been a few minor hitches here and there, but overall his troops had swept smoothly through the quarter, planting disorder and destruction wherever they went.

The werewolves would regret harassing Klaus's business interests, but payback wasn't over. Now that his army had proved to be a match for the Collado pack, they could move forward with Klaus's real agenda: clearing the werewolves out of New Orleans for good.

They had earned a celebration, and no one knew how to unwind after a fight better than a Mikaelson. Klaus had taken over the Southern Spot and his vampires had settled in with every intention of celebrating through the night.

"Did you see that one man's face when we burst in?" José laughed, his blue eyes hazy with liquor. "You'd think he'd never seen a vampire before."

"He didn't expect to see any in his bedroom, I'd wager," a former dockworker agreed, raising his glass in yet another toast.

"If not, he should have," Klaus muttered, not bothering to raise his voice. It was ridiculous for the werewolves to think they could get away with their petty little raids and that Klaus wouldn't retaliate.

"Isn't it strange that they weren't prepared at all?" Lisette asked, leaning forward to rest her elbows on her knees. He gave her a glare—she was already on his bad side. Did she need to stir up more trouble? Ignoring his look, she continued, "Klaus, I'm serious. Don't you think this was all a little bit . . . easy?"

"Spoken like a woman who spent the whole night prowling around the edges of the fighting," an ex-pickpocket sniped. She was a scrappy little slip of a thing, so fast and light on her feet that Klaus had barely caught her making off with his purse. Anna, he thought her name was, and her animosity toward Lisette raised her a notch or two in his estimation.

"Cleaning up after you children," Lisette corrected, flipping a loose lock of hair away from her freckled face. "*Literally* putting out your fires. But that's not even what I mean, which you'd have realized if you weren't in such a hurry to interrupt."

Klaus chuckled and held out his glass. A man leaped up to refill it, but knocked over the table in his drunkenness, spilling a dozen glasses all over the crowd. They were sloshed enough that they shouted good-natured protests before wandering off in search of fresh liquor.

"So what was your point, Lisette?" Klaus sighed, knowing that she would insist on telling him either way.

She played with a lock of her hair, and Klaus suppressed the impulse to rip it off her scalp. "They've been harassing you for weeks now," Lisette explained. "Stepping up their aggression and building toward an open confrontation, right? So why were they so unready for a fight when it actually came?"

A pleasantly plump young whore settled herself into Lisette's lap, and Lisette pushed her away in irritation. "This way, love," Klaus suggested, pulling the girl across his own knees. She began to unbutton his shirt, teasing at his chest with one dimpled finger. "The werewolves thought we were weak," he explained to Lisette, more patiently now that some of his needs were being attended to. "There was no way for them to know what I had prepared."

"No way?" Lisette scoffed. "Unless they'd ever met you, you mean? Klaus, no one in their right mind comes after you without expecting retaliation."

It was a valid point, if he were to assume that the werewolves were rational, thinking beings. They hadn't exactly demonstrated any of that by attacking Klaus's business interests, and yet Lisette's argument nagged at him all the same. When *had* the Collado pack grown so exceptionally idiotic?

"That's not all," Lisette went on, seizing on Klaus's hesitation. "Klaus, where was your brother tonight?" She lowered her voice, as if she could keep a room full of vampires from eavesdropping. "We both know he would never have approved of this little foray—"

"We *know*?" Klaus interrupted. "When was the last deep, meaningful talk you've had with my dear brother, Lisette?" The whore giggled, her flesh jiggling in all sorts of interesting ways.

Lisette flushed and then grew even paler than usual, her freckles standing out vividly against her porcelain skin. "I know him," she insisted. "You do, too, Klaus, and you know it's strange that he wasn't here tonight. He should have come bursting in to stop you—to stop us, I mean."

He raised an eyebrow at the revealing mistake, but didn't bother to comment on it. "Are you asking me where Elijah was tonight?" he asked. "Is that your real question, love?"

"No, I—" Lisette stuttered for a moment, then drew in a deep, shuddering breath. Somewhere across the room came the splintering sound of cracking furniture, and another good-natured shout went up from Klaus's soldiers. "I'm talking about where he *wasn't*, not where he was."

"I'm not my brother's keeper." Klaus shrugged. His whore had moved her attentions somewhat lower, and it was becoming more difficult to care about tormenting his brother's ex-lover. "It's none of my business how Elijah spent his night, or whom with. But if you're concerned about his priorities—that maybe he's gotten distracted from you and even from me—you're free to ask him about that yourself."

Lisette turned away from Klaus, but he'd already caught the glint of tears in her eyes. "You know I can't do that," she whispered, and then the windows exploded into a thousand shards of flying glass.

The vampires scattered, shouting drunken and

conflicting orders to each other. More than a few of them seemed to believe that the sun had already risen, and fled from the burning light that was still hours away. Only Klaus remained exactly where he was, waiting impatiently for whomever dared to disturb his party.

The brick that had flown through the window landed harmlessly at his feet, and Klaus nudged it away with a toe. The lantern-jawed face of Sampson Collado peered through the broken window. William Collado's son had taken his father's place as pack leader at the tender age of twenty, and while he seemed competent enough to rule during peacetime, Klaus had no doubt he could crush the young pup when it came to war.

"Come out and explain yourself, Klaus Mikaelson," the brawny werewolf ordered. "If we have to come in after you, we won't spare your people."

"If I get up from this chair, none of you will walk away from this place," Klaus countered, checking his glass hopefully. The whiskey was gone, and both the bottle and his whore had vanished somewhere in the commotion—yet another insult the wolf had to answer for.

"You owe us an explanation," Sampson growled, although Klaus noticed that he made no move to enter the brothel. "We've upheld the peace in this city for twenty-two years, only to be attacked in the night by your band of cowards. I want to know why you chose this night to break our treaty."

"To save you the trouble of breaking it in the morning," Klaus said. "You've been harassing my businesses for weeks now, and I know all about your planned attack for tomorrow. I have eyes and ears everywhere, you young fool."

Sampson took a step back from the window frame, but with a smirk on his face that indicated he was in no way retreating. "Bring the human," he called back to his comrades, and two of the werewolves dragged forward a man who had been beaten to within an inch of his life.

Both of his eyes were swollen shut, and his nose and one cheekbone had been badly broken. But all the same, Klaus recognized Guillaume, the spy who had been keeping tabs on the werewolves' insurrection for him. "How dare you?" he shouted, jumping to his feet at last. Some of the bruises on Guillaume's face were hours old—they must have been working him over since the raid.

"Tell him what you told us," Sampson ordered, shoving Guillaume roughly. "Skip the part where we had to torture it out of you, because no one wants this little parlay to last that long."

Guillaume coughed, and Klaus could hear the telltale sound of internal injuries. If the man lived to see the next day, it would be his last. Becoming a vampire could save his life, but Klaus had no further need of a spy who was stupid enough to get caught by werewolves.

"I'm sorry," Guillaume wheezed. "I'm so—"

One of the werewolves shook him violently, and Guillaume's tobacco-stained teeth rattled in his skull. "I'm sure you're *deeply* sorry," Klaus assured his informant, stepping closer to the broken window, "at least to have gotten caught, you idiot." Guillaume's bloodshot eyes followed Klaus's movements a second too late, and one of his pupils was noticeably larger than the other. "But you can make it right by telling me what else you're sorry for."

"It wasn't the wolves," Guillaume gasped, just before his body was racked by another round of guttural coughing. "I met a man in a tavern. He had gold, and he said you'd be attacked. He said it would be best if you thought the werewolves did it, and he had gold."

His head lolled toward his chest, and Klaus slapped him smartly across the face. "Tell me about this man," he snapped. "Was he a vampire, or a witch? What name did he use?"

"Human," Guillaume rasped. "Just human. He said the city used to be *ours*, and it should be again. He said you could all kill each other and the humans could take back their home."

"A name," Klaus growled. There were tens of thousands of humans in New Orleans. Klaus wasn't opposed to killing them all just to be on the safe side, but that wouldn't leave him much of a city to rule.

"I don't have one, but he had black hair and tanned skin. A gentleman," the miserable spy groaned, and in spite of his own fury Klaus believed him. Sampson gave a nod, confirming that the same answer had been given under torture. "He isn't working alone," Guillaume wheezed, and the werewolf and Klaus both straightened attentively.

"Tell us what he told you," Sampson urged, his deep voice almost gentle. He must have been able to hear Guillaume's imminent death as clearly as Klaus could, and was changing his tactics to suit the occasion.

Guillaume swallowed hard, his Adam's apple sliding around in his throat. "He said he has weapons. The type that work against your kind—he works as a merchant, and he has spent a lot of time and money collecting those things. I never asked for a name, and he didn't give it. But I could pick out some of his friends in the tavern, pretending to be strangers—I was surrounded. He wore a cloak pin, and there were men and women there wearing the same design. On pins, embroidered into the design of a dress, one had it drawn into her skin. Two faces, looking out in opposite ways from the same head."

"Janus," Klaus frowned. "A Roman god with twin faces, looking at the past and the future at once. Could that have been his name, perhaps, or is it some other conceit?"

"I don't—" Guillaume coughed again, and Klaus waved dismissively.

"Never mind, he's spent. Sampson, I think we have much to discuss." Klaus stepped back from the window, and Sampson gestured to his werewolves to drag Guillaume away. Klaus had no idea how they would dispose of the traitor, and he didn't care. It would seem that he had other humans to deal with.

Sampson rested one hand on the windowsill and then jumped over it, landing lightly on the other side. He was an inch or two shorter than Klaus, with a square, solid build that matched his broadly handsome face. Klaus found a bottle of whiskey that was, miraculously, neither broken nor empty, and he set it on the table. The two men sat, appraising each other. One of the terrified Southern Spot girls poured the amber liquid with a trembling hand.

"So," Klaus began, ignoring the shamefaced vampires who had begun to quietly file back to their seats. "Some humans have gone to a great deal of trouble to set us at each other's throats. I don't see us ever becoming friends, but there's no denying we have a common enemy."

Sampson sipped his whiskey and then smiled, and for a moment Klaus thought he detected a hint of yellow in the depths of his brown eyes. "Too bad for that enemy, then."

EIGHT

Rebekah laid Luc's convulsing body among the roots of the White Oak tree, her own hands shaking. She wasn't going to let Tomás get away, and there was no more time to lose. His back was already disappearing into the darkness.

She overtook him by a stand of pine trees, just where the woods grew thick and dark. Bad enough that he had threatened her, and even worse that he'd hurt Luc, but walking away from an Original was unforgivable.

Tomás didn't turn to confront her, but he didn't flee, either. Rebekah caught the edge of his black cloak and spun him around to face her. "So nice to see you again so soon. How's your lover doing?" he asked, leering a little. "I'm surprised you left him all by himself in these woods. Don't you know there are predators out here?"

"What did you do to him?" Rebekah demanded. "What was that powder, and who gave it to you?"

Tomás's laughter was sudden and sharp. "You think I'll help you, Rebekah? I stood before your greatest weakness and told you I would destroy you. Do you always cling so to your enemies? No wonder you're a thousand-year-old spinster still living with your brothers."

Rebekah took a menacing step forward, so she was close enough to see every plane and shadow of his face. He had a high-bridged nose and sharply angled cheekbones. His face looked haughty and superior without even trying, and so when he smirked at her, the effect was especially condescending. "You seem to think you know a lot about me," she purred, eyeing him up and down cautiously. He made no move for his weapon, but he had already surprised her once. "Then you know I'm not afraid of parlor tricks or empty threats."

Tomás's voice was a low hiss. "I know what you *are* afraid of, Rebekah."

Unable to stop herself, she lashed out, striking at his smug mouth as if she could force those ugly words back inside. But her fist connected with nothing but air, and

Rebekah almost lost her balance from the force of the blow. Tomás had moved faster than a human should have been able to—almost as fast as a vampire.

She spun to face him and shot out one leg, knocking his feet out from under him. He rolled and pulled himself up to a wary crouch before she could press her advantage.

"Tell me who you are," she said.

"Merely a concerned citizen," he answered, his pale green eyes sparkling with some private joke. Then he spread his hands wide, indicating the forest and the little town on the other side of the trees. "Does this feel like your home, Rebekah? You've lived nearly eighty years in my city, but you were human here. Does that make a difference to a monster like you?"

"I *am* a monster," she agreed, fed up with trying to make sense of the bizarre twists of his mind. Wind creaked in the branches overhead and stirred her hair around her shoulders. "I have no feelings, no attachments. Nothing here or anywhere means anything to me, so just undo whatever you did to Luc and be on your way. You picked the wrong monster to try to hurt."

Tomás slowly stood up from his crouch, his tall body unfolding like a skeleton. "I would like to believe you're telling the truth," he mused. "It would be easier to understand how someone with no feelings could commit all of the evil acts you have to answer for. But you care about that good-looking lump of a vampire you left under the White Oak tree, and I believe you care about your home as well. But where is it you really belong? The place you lived as a child, or the mansion you occupied while you destroyed *my* home?"

"Your home?" Rebekah knew she needed to remain in control, but she was genuinely shocked. Tomás had accumulated strength and power, had learned about her history, and had attacked her lover, all over something so trivial she could hardly believe it. "You're a human; the entire world is your home. You're like grains of sand, drifting in and filling up every last crevice. I haven't taken anything from you that can't easily be replaced."

"I might say the same of that Luc fellow." Tomás shrugged. "Perhaps there are so many of us that you can't tell humans apart anymore, but I came of age in a city your family ruled. The Mikaelsons have lived off the backs and blood of humanity for far too long now, and I intend to stop you."

"With witches' tricks?" Rebekah scoffed, feinting at his head and body a few times. Tomás blocked or avoided each blow, then landed an unexpectedly forceful kick in the center of her abdomen.

"I have tricks even they don't know," he warned, and Rebekah believed him.

If it was true that Tomás *was* just an ordinary human citizen of New Orleans, how had he come to be so powerful? Rebekah and her kind had spent decades happily feeding off the city's residents, never dreaming that the humans might find a way to fight back. Now she was forced to wonder how many of them had already sided with Tomás.

The longer they fought, at least, the better she understood his method. She was confident that she could crush the life out of Tomás if she really wanted to, but first she need to know how to cure Luc, as well as how far this insurrection had spread. Tomás knew too much to be working alone.

"An uprising will cost you more than you can pay," she warned. "And even if you succeeded in toppling us, whatever moved in in our place might be worse. Humans were meant to be ruled, and you'll never go long without a new boot on your necks."

"So it might as well be yours?" Tomás taunted. Rebekah caught a glimpse of movement in the darkness behind him, and she realized that their sparring had led them back toward the White Oak tree. Luc was still immobile at its trunk, his blue eyes fixed on nothing. "I think we can do better."

She lunged forward, but something happened as she closed in on Tomás—a flicker, a blur. She saw it coming, but there was nothing she could do: Her momentum carried her forward into the cloud of powder that he had blown into her face.

It burned. It burned so badly that she couldn't move or even think, and everything around her disappeared except for the pain. She might as well have swallowed pure sunlight, and she could feel it boiling her from the inside out. Rebekah froze in place, her hands straining at her throat.

"Stay here by your tree awhile," she heard Tomás say, somewhere close by in the blackness. He sounded near enough to touch, and Rebekah fought against the magic that surrounded her with every ounce of strength she possessed. "Think over what I've said. The next time you see me, I will have taken even more of what you love."

Tomás's lips pressed against hers and lingered . . . making her feel so dizzy in her blindness that she no longer knew if her feet were still on the ground. He deserved to die for that stolen kiss alone, but she couldn't move so much as a finger.

As her vision began to return, Rebekah could see Tomás walking away from her again. *Again*. She should have slaughtered him when she had the chance. It had been beneath her to trade insults with him, to even bother trying to understand his intentions. He should never have lived so long, nor gotten so close. Rebekah needed to fix her mistake. No matter what tricks Tomás had up his sleeve, she was an Original.

She could map out every step it would take to reach him. She knew exactly where her feet would land, and she could imagine the earth springing back up beneath them. But no matter what she did or how hard she tried, Rebekah couldn't force her body to actually move toward Tomás.

The powder wasn't only painful, she realized: It was controlling her. The last words he had spoken to her were no mere suggestion. Tomás had ordered her to remain beneath the tree, and his horrible trick had compelled her to obey. When she was able to move at last, it was only to step backward, toward the tree and Luc's prone body. Every time she decided to follow Tomás her muscles locked themselves in place again, frozen while she burned.

He had turned the tables on her, she realized. Tomás had objected to the vampires' rule over his city, and now he was establishing a rule of his own over vampires. It was a perversion of the natural order of things, and it made him far more than the petty annoyance she had believed him to be at first. But until the spell wore off there was nothing Rebekah could do except take care of Luc, who still shivered in the throes of the same searing pain.

Luc's eyes were open a little, but they stared into nothing. Rebekah brushed back some of his blond hair that had slipped loose and fallen across his face, and even that small movement made her feel light-headed.

The pain was easing a bit, but a strange numbness was flooding Rebekah's limbs in its place, and she was beginning to see more stars than just the ones in the sky. She fought against the heaviness of her eyelids for as long as she could, but she could tell it was a losing battle.

She awoke curled protectively around Luc's body, as if to shield him from whatever dangers still lurked around the White Oak tree. The crescent moon winked at her, much lower in the sky than it had been before. Hours had passed, and Rebekah seethed at the thought of how far away Tomás had probably gotten by now.

Rebekah couldn't figure out what kind of magic he had used. She had never heard of a substance like this one, and Tomás had enough of it to throw around. As she looked up at the moon, Rebekah thought about what this meant for her and her loved ones. Tomás had promised to destroy everything she loved, and for the first time Rebekah had to consider the possibility that he might actually have that kind of power at his disposal.

She had come to Mystic Falls seeking the means to kill Klaus, full of the conviction that he was a danger to all she held dear. But the world had always been full of dangers for her, and the one she had discovered tonight might be even more urgent than the one that had brought her here in the first place. Klaus was violent and erratic, truly a loose cannon—but he was still family. Tomás had the air of menace that came from having a plan, and from possessing the means to carry it out.

Luc stirred, and Rebekah straightened, focusing all her attention on him. He'd been unconscious much longer than she had, and she could only imagine how much pain he must be in.

"It's all right," she murmured, resting a cool hand on his tanned cheek. "I'm here."

Luc groaned, and his eyes went wide. He looked at her and grabbed her wrist, twisting it away from his face. He sprang to his feet so quickly that Rebekah was knocked backward, landing among the twisting roots. He stared at her for a moment, squinting as if he could barely make her out.

"Luc?" she asked, unsure if he could hear her. She held her hands up, palms out, hoping to calm him, but he trembled violently, and she could see sweat beading on his forehead, even in the cool night.

"Abomination," he rasped, and she could almost hear Tomás's voice speaking to her through Luc's familiar lips. The planes of his face were hard and drawn, and there was a hollow look in his eyes.

"We were bewitched," Rebekah told him carefully, waiting for him to recognize her voice. "It's going to be all right, Luc—this will pass."

A deep, bone-rattling shudder passed through his body, and then he sprang at her, every trace of his confusion and stiffness vanishing in an instant. He landed a crushing blow on her left temple, then lifted her by her throat and threw her against the tree trunk.

Rebekah felt her teeth snap over her tongue and tasted blood. Luc bared his fangs and rushed at her again, and she could see pure madness glowing in his bright blue eyes.

It had to be the powder—more of Tomás's mind control. Rebekah couldn't bear the thought of killing Luc over something that he couldn't help. But she still had to fight, and so she blocked his next attack with enough force to send him flying through the air.

He crashed to his knees on the grass a hundred yards away, but he kept his eyes riveted on Rebekah the entire time. He circled sideways, watching her for any opening or sign of weakness.

"This won't last forever," she promised him. "The pain will pass, and you'll realize who I am—who *you* are." Rebekah felt nearly like her old self again already, as if each breath she took cleared the last traces of the powder from her body. Luc might not be as strong as she was, but eventually he would shake off the spell.

Luc snarled at the sound of her voice, as if every reminder of her existence enraged him.

"Come, then!" Rebekah shouted at him, losing her patience. "If we're meant to fight, let's fight."

Luc crouched and then sprang, reminding her of a lion in the middle of a hunt, his golden hair waving loose around his shoulders. She twisted out of the way just as he reached her, and Luc staggered, holding the gnarled tree trunk for support. And then he reached up and caught one of the White Oak's lower branches. "This is what we came here for, isn't it?" he asked, and she heard the sound of splintering wood. Realizing her mistake, Rebekah ran at him, but it was too late: The branch snapped off in his hand, the stake's jagged point aimed straight for her heart.

Rebekah turned just enough to catch the stake in her shoulder. It felt like an icicle tearing through her flesh, but she ignored the pain and wrenched her shoulder back, hoping to surprise Luc enough that he would lose his grip on the branch.

Instead he shifted it the opposite way, a tight smile playing on his lips as he forced the wound open wider. "And to think that I once thought you were invincible," he hissed. "Now I can't imagine how you've managed to live this long."

Rebekah heard some small bone in her shoulder break, and she felt panic rising in her chest. She swung wildly at Luc's face with her good arm, unable to form any coherent goal except to get the stake out of her body and away from her. She heard him grunt and felt a satisfying pop as his nose burst into a fountain of blood.

He punched her back, and she blocked the blow only to see his eyes shift. It was just a distraction from the real threat: the stake. While Rebekah knocked aside his right hand, his left fist drove the stake toward her heart.

Rebekah forced her left arm to catch Luc's wrist, and she bent it back, twisting so hard that she heard a snap. He bellowed in pain, and his fingers spasmed around the rough wood. Rebekah watched her own fingers close around the branch, and she gritted her teeth against the pain in her shoulder as she gripped the stake as hard as she could. She wrested it from his grasp and then slashed the jagged end across his cheekbone. Luc stumbled back and Rebekah pressed her advantage, slicing viciously at his face and body as he struggled to defend every part of himself at once.

She could barely see the wounds she inflicted through the fury that all but blinded her. Would she never learn? She had meant to spare Luc's life, and that sentiment had put her in mortal danger. Luc was a pleasant enough lover, and along their journey she had imagined that they might truly grow close, but he wasn't worth her life. Especially when he wasn't even himself anymore.

Luc faltered under her onslaught, and the roots of the White Oak tree caught at his feet, tripping him. Rebekah drove her knee up into the pit of his stomach as he wavered, and he fell heavily to the ground. She was on him in the blink of an eye, one knee on either side of his hips. "This is how I've survived, you son of a bitch," she told him, her voice hoarse and rasping from the exertion of the fight.

Luc's eyes widened in surprise when he saw his stake in her hand, positioned just above his own racing heart. The alarm on his face reached her even through the haze of her anger, and she hesitated, still hoping against hope that she might not need to use the stake. But if she waited too long, the sun would rise above the trees around them and take the decision out of her hands.

"Hurry up and come back to me," she whispered urgently, hating her own lingering doubt as much as his stubborn inability to shake off the effects of Tomás's powder. "There's just no more time for this."

"Rebekah?" he said, and she could feel his body relax ever so slightly beneath hers. "Is that—? I can't see you." His voice was softer, less certain, with none of the cold hatred it had held before.

"I'm here," she answered, leaning back a little. It seemed almost too lucky to be true. But magic was nothing if not capricious, and above all else Rebekah *wanted* to believe. "Luc, you need to shake this off now. That man did something to you, but it's going to be all right."

"That man," he repeated, and he lifted his head a little as if he was trying to find her. "Are you still there, Rebekah?"

The sounds of his voice broke her heart. He had been so strong, so vibrant and vital, and it was almost physically painful to see him reduced to this. "I'm here," she repeated, reaching out with her free hand to touch the side of his face.

He struck like a viper, whipping his hand around her other wrist and twisting it brutally. The White

Oak stake fell from her hand and clattered away among the roots. She dove for it.

"You really are a fool for love." Luc's boot struck Rebekah hard in the lower back just as her fingers closed on the stake, and she tasted blood and earth as she collapsed face-first on the ground. She rolled to face him, but Luc ignored her and aimed his next kick at the stake. It flew out of her hand again, and she couldn't see where it landed.

He hit her just as she jumped to her feet, a crushing backhanded blow that sent her spinning against the trunk of the tree, stars exploding behind her eyes. Rebekah blinked, trying to clear her head, but it was too late. The next thing she saw was Luc looming before her, the broken branch in his hand once again.

He didn't hesitate. Luc brought the stake down straight and true. It slid between Rebekah's ribs at a perfect angle and pierced her heart as if it were coming home.

NINE

*E*lijah found himself walking down the narrow street that led to the Southern Spot, a pit in his stomach. He had to know if it was true—was his own brother truly plotting against him? It wouldn't be the first time Klaus had sought to undermine one of his brothers.

But Klaus conspiring with the Collado pack? Didn't he still blame them for the death of Vivianne Lescheres? Klaus wasn't the type of man who forgave easily, although he was known to let go of a grudge when it benefited him.

Away from the alluring sight of Alejandra and the persuasive sound of her voice, Elijah thought over what she'd told him. It was possible that her information was wrong—a terrible misunderstanding. But she was a very intelligent woman, and if she had believed such a wild tale it must have sounded convincing. Elijah hoped that he and Klaus could sort it out over a few tankards of ale and then resume their balance of power.

One of the brothel's windows was smashed and glass littered the cobblestones, glinting in the predawn light. Anyone could have broken the window, but the timing was too coincidental for it to have been a drunken accident. Elijah moved closer, silently crossing the empty lane and checking to make sure no one was watching. It was strangely quiet on the street—nothing stirred in the early hour, no drunks tumbled out onto the street, no liquored-up brawls reached his ears.

Had they gone to celebrate somewhere else? Or worse, was this a trap, and were they waiting for him? He crept closer. The voices inside the Southern Spot were so low that he couldn't distinguish them until he reached the broken window. But once at the window ledge, he immediately recognized one of the speakers.

Klaus was there, just as Alejandra had said he would be, but that didn't mean that the rest of her information was accurate. The brothel was usually the best place to look for Klaus.

Then the other man spoke. Elijah closed his eyes for

a moment. Half a dozen small, unimportant mysteries came together to form a brand-new truth. Sampson Collado was sitting inside the Southern Spot, proof that Klaus hated his own brother more than he hated his ancient enemies.

"—been pulling all our strings," Sampson was saying. "Truth be told, I'm surprised you went along with it for so long."

"For the sake of our new friendship, I'll pretend you didn't say that," Klaus drawled. "I had good reasons for what I did, and better reasons for what I will do next."

"Fair enough," Sampson agreed, and Elijah could hear that the wolf was in no way intimidated by Klaus. Apparently the two of them were getting along quite well—far better than Elijah expected. "But you won't be doing it alone. We're talking about someone who has resources, connections, and a plan. You and I act in the moment, but he's looking at a much bigger picture."

"A plan is no match for a hearty dose of chaos," Klaus said, and Elijah could picture the sardonic way his jaw shifted sideways as he said it. "I would think that this meeting alone is already a substantial change to the big picture."

"I doubt an alliance between the two of us is

something anyone would have foreseen," Sampson rumbled appreciatively.

The room around them was full of rustling sounds, clearing throats, glasses tapping on tables. Two armies sat waiting on their generals, ready for the moment when the orders were handed down.

Elijah knew that he should be patient, learn more, choose his moment carefully. History had proven Klaus wrong time and again: A couple of hotheads didn't stand a chance against someone with a vision. But when Klaus chuckled and Elijah heard their glasses clink together in a toast, he couldn't stop himself.

Elijah leapt through the window, landing in a crouch on the unpolished floorboards. "My brother and I are going to need the room," he growled.

Lisette's clear gray eyes locked onto his and held them for an extra moment. Elijah kept his expression perfectly still, but it cost him nearly all his self-control. No matter how angry she had grown at him, no matter how bitter his rejection had made her, he had never expected her betrayal to hurt this much.

Lisette opened her mouth to speak, but Elijah had no desire to hear her excuses; he only wanted her out of his sight as quickly as possible. "Go!" he bellowed, and vampires and werewolves scattered for the doors.

Lisette moved slower than the rest, lingering as if

she hoped Elijah would call for her. He didn't, and he hoped that she shared some small measure of his pain in that moment.

Last to leave was Sampson, who cast a meaningful glance in Klaus's direction. It was as if the two of them could communicate without words, as if they had a shared history that let them understand each other with just a look. It was as if somehow, while Elijah's attention had been elsewhere, Sampson and Klaus had become brothers.

"Elijah," Klaus cheered, and for the first time Elijah noticed that he was profoundly, prodigiously drunk. He didn't slur his words, but Elijah knew him well enough to notice the subtler signs. Klaus's blue-green eyes were unnaturally bright, and they tracked Elijah's movements just a fraction of a second too slowly.

Klaus's body was relaxed, draped over his chair with one leg casually extended in front of him. Elijah stepped in close, ready to intimidate his brother back into submission. "Don't toy with me, brother," Elijah warned. "No need for any of your lies. I always believed, no matter how outrageous your behavior, that in the end we were on the same side, but now I understand that you have never felt the same way."

"It was just a little raid," Klaus scoffed, swirling the last dregs of whiskey in his glass. He glanced around, and Elijah realized that he was looking for a new bottle. There wasn't one within reach and he was obviously disinclined to get up from his chair. "The werewolves started it. They didn't start it, I mean, so we're all good friends now."

"You're even more drunk than I thought," Elijah muttered, honestly surprised that Klaus had let himself get so incoherent. Klaus was self-indulgent, but he had also always been naturally wary. If he had lowered his guard so far while drinking with the Collado pack, their alliance must be secure indeed. "Did all that whiskey dull the shame of turning your back on your family?"

"I have nothing to be ashamed of!" Klaus shouted, his chin jutting out belligerently. It was enough to make Elijah miss how Rebekah handled Klaus. "If anyone has turned his back, it's you. You sit perched up there on your imaginary throne, ignoring everything else as long as you can call yourself ruler. No one holds on to power forever, dear brother, unless he's willing to fight for it."

Elijah aimed an expert kick at the legs of Klaus's chair, splintering three of them with one solid blow. The chair collapsed and Klaus fell with it. He swayed to his feet with less than his usual speed. "You're in no shape to fight me," Elijah spat, "but that doesn't mean I'm not willing."

Klaus bared his fangs, and Elijah didn't hesitate; he closed his fist and hit his brother in the mouth with every ounce of his extraordinary strength. It felt fantastic, even when Klaus snarled and threw a nearby table at Elijah's face in return.

Elijah grabbed his brother by the throat, and Klaus dragged at his hands, trying to break their iron grip. The two vampires fell to the ground, still struggling for purchase as they wrestled among the shards of broken glass and cracked bottles.

Klaus gained the advantage for a moment, twisting across Elijah's body. Elijah rolled out of the way just in time, but Klaus's leg shot out and tangled with his, tripping him. Elijah shoved, kneed, and punched, brawling with his little brother like they had when they were teenagers.

He didn't have the hatred in him to kill Klaus, he realized. Elijah had known for centuries which of them was the better man, and there was no need to prove it. All he had ever wanted was Klaus's loyalty, and he was beginning to understand that he was never going to get it.

He threw Klaus across the room and stood, dusting off his wrinkled coat in disgust. "Stay down," he snapped when Klaus began to pull himself to his feet, and although Klaus didn't obey, he made no move to resume their fight.

Fighting had been pointless, anyway: It was always pointless. Elijah and his brother could spend the next year beating each other's heads in, and still neither of them would ever win. Maybe it really was time to go their separate ways. Elijah could certainly think of a few things he would rather do than worry about Klaus all the time.

"We're done here," a voice said, and Elijah was startled to realize it was his own. "Do whatever you want with the city, Niklaus. It's yours. We're done."

Elijah turned and walked out of the brothel, letting the door slam behind him. He could see the first orange streaks of sunrise in the eastern sky, and daybreak had never seemed so appropriate. The future itself was opening before Elijah, full of more possibilities and fewer obligations than Elijah could remember facing in his entire life.

Alejandra had been right, and the first thing he intended to do was find her and tell her so. She had seen what he could not: that Klaus and Rebekah didn't think they needed him. Both of them believed that they would be happier if they forged their own way.

And at long last, Elijah was free to do the same.

TEN

*K*laus and his army raced against the rising sun. There was only half an hour left before they'd be forced to take cover, but thanks to Lisette's clever idea, the long daylight hours didn't have to be wasted. Not as long as they got to their destination. Klaus stormed through the cobblestoned streets, his soldiers following at his heels.

"I don't understand why you didn't just tell him—" Lisette began again, hurrying alongside Klaus as his second-in-command. Her promotion would either be short lived, or Klaus would have to start tolerating her presence—depending on whether her plan worked.

"He wasn't willing to listen," Klaus snapped. "Elijah

always has to be in charge, and he couldn't handle hearing that he had fallen out of touch with his city. The bastard can be surprisingly sensitive, as you know."

"He takes on a lot," Lisette argued, jogging to keep pace with Klaus's long strides. "If he had our support, instead of—"

"We're saving New Orleans for him," Klaus reminded her sharply. "If he ever humbles enough to notice, he has all the support he could ask for. But instead of asking, he barged in and acted like a lunatic, so I don't really care *what* he thinks of us right now. I can't worry about his precious feelings when I have to get on with doing his job for him."

"That's not really—"

"Shut *up*," Klaus ordered. Learning to put up with Lisette might be even more difficult than he thought. "I told you, he didn't want to listen. I would think that you, of all people, would know what that's like."

His vampires coursed through the streets, moving on ahead of them, and Klaus fed off their impatience. The city jail was just a few blocks away, on the western outskirts of New Orleans. Sampson Collado had brought Klaus a problem, and Klaus's solution was an unstoppable army. And what better place to recruit soldiers than a prison? It was full of citizens who could use a second chance at making a meaningful contribution to their city. He had Lisette to thank for that genius idea.

If the Cult of Janus was as well connected and supplied as Guillaume had claimed, then all Klaus needed was more vampires. With enough men he could cut off their supply chain, infiltrate their command, and stamp out their little insurgence.

Since the jail was nearly windowless, Klaus's army could spend the day there, turning all the prisoners into new vampires, and by the time the next moon rose their ranks would have doubled or more. New Orleans's worst criminals would be put to work saving the city from itself, and Klaus could show Elijah just how ludicrous his behavior in the brothel had been.

No matter what his brother believed, Elijah wasn't the only vampire in the world who was capable of seeing a problem and crafting a solution. He had never given any of his siblings the credit they deserved, and especially not Klaus. He was so busy painting himself as their rescuer that he had absolutely blinded himself to the possibility that the roles might occasionally reverse.

"We'll make it with time to spare." José smirked. The slight thief seemed impressed by his own speed and endurance in the way that only a new vampire could be. Klaus remembered that feeling, of everything being new and astonishing, before his incredible power had truly become a part of him, as natural as his heartbeat.

"Of course we will," said Lisette. "Look, the Alonso brothers have reached the gate."

The brothers, a cheerful pair of former fishermen, tore off the guards' heads and pried open the heavy door. Others rushed to help, making short work of iron bars and thick, oaken boards. Klaus gave one last look over his shoulder before he slipped inside the jail. A burning sliver of the sun was just visible over the bayou, and Klaus grinned in satisfaction before turning to survey his newest recruits.

The Spanish were not popular rulers in New Orleans, and the jail cells were overcrowded with murderers, rebels, and fighters. Klaus wanted them all.

"They drink before they die!" Klaus shouted. His army couldn't forget their mission. The prisoners had to drink blood before they were killed, or else they wouldn't turn.

Guards were to be compelled to stand down or else killed—he had no use for them. They were tools of the Spanish government, and possible extensions of Janus's shadowy arm. Klaus saw José drinking deeply from one guard, his bright red uniform stained with the darker shade of blood. "Don't fill up just yet," Klaus reminded him, and José promptly snapped the guard's neck.

"Blood is all you'll get from us!" another guard

shouted, running at them wildly. "There will be no more of your kind polluting our city."

"Everyone's a hero until the last second," Klaus said to José, throwing the guard against a stone wall so that his skull shattered. "But when a man can look his own death right in the eye, he always drinks."

Farther along the corridor, vampires had begun opening the cells, wrenching the doors clean off their hinges. The prisoners shouted impatiently for their release, but the ones who were free could sense the danger they were in. They stayed huddled against the walls, trying to get away from the vampires. They had been criminals and convicts: They knew what hunger looked like.

"You will all drink this," one of the Alonso brothers ordered, rolling his sleeve back and opening a vein in his forearm. The prisoners cringed, and one of them gagged audibly. Klaus silently cursed Alonso's clumsiness, and he had to resist the urge to kill the idiot and let the others try their luck. The fisherman had been human mere days ago, and yet apparently had already forgotten how repugnant humans would find the idea of drinking blood.

The prisoners stared at the blood for a moment, then looked at each other. At that silent cue, they rushed at the vampire together.

Chaos erupted as other prisoners followed their lead, charging the vampires who stood between them and a chance at freedom. Klaus's soldiers were strong, but with all the humans attacking at once, they had their hands full containing the riot.

"Drink this if you want to live," Klaus heard Lisette order, and he turned toward the sound of her voice. She held her bleeding arm against a man's mouth, gripping his throat with her other hand. The man's eyes bulged in fear and disgust, but Klaus saw his throat work, and offered Lisette a terse but respectful nod. She crushed the man's windpipe like an overripe piece of fruit and discarded his corpse on the cold stone floor. "Drink this if you want to live," she repeated to the next nearest prisoner, who gaped at her in horror.

Across the corridor Klaus heard an enraged howl, and turned just in time to see one of his vampires sink his fangs into a surprised prisoner's throat. Klaus was beside the pair in a flash and dragged them apart, keeping a firm grip on both of their collars.

"The son of a bitch punched me," the vampire snarled, and Klaus could see a telltale bump where his nose had been broken.

"He *bit* me," the prisoner complained, his voice shrill with shock.

"He drinks first," Klaus reminded the sulking

vampire. "They all do, or don't bother coming back to the garrison."

He knocked their heads together—not *too* hard, since it wouldn't do to kill the prisoner yet—and moved on through the melee. All the cells had been opened at last, and the screams rang merrily through the building. Klaus took careful note of which of his soldiers required his intervention, and which seemed to be learning quickly enough on the job.

Over the next hour, the long vaulted corridor grew quieter. The layer of bodies on the floor was so thick that it was almost impossible to walk from one end to the other without stepping on a hand or a limp leg. Sunlight scattered across the carnage, but the jail wasn't intended to feel light or airy, and it was easy to avoid the rays. They'd accomplished a good morning's work.

"José," he called, catching sight of the man. The thief looked the part of a dangerous warrior at last, smeared with the blood of a dozen dead men. "The guards must have kept a stash of liquor around here somewhere. See if you can find it, would you?"

José hurried along the passageway and disappeared through the far door. Klaus leaned against a stone wall and watched the last few humans die.

They remained there for the day, drunk on blood and growing even more inebriated with the help of a few casks of wine José had discovered in the cellar. The tiny patches of sunlight moved across the floor, and vampires played and sparred around them, daring and taunting one another to stand as close as they could bear before their skin started to sizzle. They brawled and sang while the sun passed overhead, then sank on the jail's western side.

"Move the bodies out," Klaus ordered when the sun was finally low enough, and dozens of lazy, intoxicated faces turned his way in surprise. "Move!" he shouted, and vampires began scrambling to their feet. "To the mansion, I think." It was closer than his garrison, and they were less likely to be disturbed by any overeager rebel.

His army, shouldering their newest recruits, filed out into the twilight and slipped into the woods that bordered the jail, taking the long way home. The mansion lay to the northwest of them. Even with each of them carrying two bodies at a time, they would all have to make multiple trips, and they would have to hurry to finish by moonrise.

Klaus left them to it, strolling alone toward his mansion in the growing darkness. The cobblestoned streets were just as deserted as they had been at dawn. He hadn't noticed until now just how mindful the citizenry had become of his kind and their feeding habits. The humans of New Orleans knew all about vampires, and they kept to their homes at night.

He rounded a corner and stopped, blinking in surprise at a white mark that had been painted onto the side of a butcher shop. It was one head with two faces, each looking in opposite directions: the symbol of Janus. The symbol was like cold fingers creeping up Klaus's back. The cult had grown bold, riling up the population and putting their stamp on the city.

Klaus shook himself, shoving those gloomy thoughts aside. He had an army now, and no one was going to stop him from ruling New Orleans.

He imagined that his soldiers had finally reached the mansion. He could picture them rolling the corpses onto the fine carpets and smooth marble floors, their blood ruining—or enhancing?—Rebekah's priceless collection. Hundreds of freshly dead bodies would soon begin to twitch and breathe, and Klaus would use them to make his own mark on the city.

He rested his hands behind his head, whistling cheerfully as he made his way toward home.

ELEVEN

As the White Oak stake found her heart, Rebekah screamed in pain, never having felt such misery before. It was as if her heart were breaking a million times over. She felt her eyes go wide and then shut tight, but she didn't stop seeing. She could still picture the tree, its image seared into the darkness behind her eyes. There was daylight, and children who ran and played beneath its broad leaves. She could see little Klaus's sardonic smile and Elijah's warm brown eyes and even the flowers woven into her own hair. Their other brothers were there as well: Kol and Finn and tiny Henrik.

There was no danger, no threats waiting on the horizon. There was nothing but hope.

Rebekah ran to her family's cottage and saw her mother, the most beautiful woman in the world, stirring something in a steaming pot on the hearth. Esther stood and smiled, in the comforting way she always did, and Rebekah wondered if she had flown into her mother's arms that day, or if she had simply run to taste the stew. She could see both events, as if her past had been placed between two mirrors that stretched off forever in both directions, but showed two different lives. If she had hugged her mother that day, would she have become a vampire? What small decisions had led her to this endless path?

Mikael swung her up onto his shoulders, striding through a wide field while she giggled and twined her hands in his hair. There was no sign of the villain he would become. He was just her father: tall and strong and impossibly wise, showing her the world she had once believed she would live and die in.

They were all there, together and happy, as if the tree had been holding on to some part of the Mikaelsons for all those centuries. The tree belonged to them, and Rebekah realized she had been wrong to fear it for so long. It wasn't destroying her like she always believed it would. Instead, the stake in her heart was restoring the life that should have been hers. A real human life—with a beginning, an end, and a family who loved her.

Rebekah could hear her mother calling to her. But Esther had died centuries before, and if she called to her daughter, then she had to be calling from the Other Side. She wanted Rebekah to go to her, to join her there at last.

"My child," Esther whispered, and Rebekah strained to hear her voice over the buzzing of insects and the chirping of birds in the sunlight. "My darling child, you have lost your way in the night."

Rebekah blinked, and in the second her eyes closed, she could see the full horror of what her mother meant. Darkness and blood and death filled all her senses, overwhelming them until her eyes flew open again. Her home was there, just where it belonged, surrounded by flowers and children and love.

"You have always belonged here," Esther told her. The words in her mother's soft, powerful voice rang true, like the truest thing Rebekah had ever been told. Rebekah could have lived and died in Mystic Falls, and her life would have been perfect.

"I want to be with my family," Rebekah told her, her voice sounding close and far away at the same time. "Death scattered us, and I've tried to hold on to all the pieces."

She blinked again and saw Marguerite, gruesomely pale, with her brown eyes staring forever at the ceiling. She felt the shock of that terrible betrayal, then the overwhelming grief of losing yet another person she thought would be by her side forever.

Marguerite would be on the Other Side now, along with Esther, Henrik, Eric, and countless other loved ones. Tomás had asked Rebekah where her home truly was; perhaps the Other Side was it.

"And I have wanted to be with you," Esther promised. "I have watched you and longed for the day you would return to me, to be reunited again."

There was a shimmering at the far end of the field, where the path led back down toward the village. Rebekah took one uncertain step toward it and then another, and Esther's voice grew stronger as she approached.

"You don't belong in that world anymore," she said, and Rebekah could feel her mother's voice pulling her. Rebekah had lived as a monster among monsters, and now she could leave that all behind. She could shed it like a worn cloak and be herself again.

There was another voice calling to her, she realized, and Rebekah paused, cocking her head to listen. It was someone wrong; someone who didn't belong in this time or place. The voice was from another life, one in which Rebekah had been motherless for centuries. Where she had lost siblings and lovers and sacrificed too many parts of herself. But it was telling her that there had been bright spots, as well. Her long life had also been full of love.

She could never have lost so much if she hadn't loved so deeply. That was worth the suffering, the voice cried, drifting to her ears from what felt like centuries away. Life was full of both pain and joy, and Rebekah had never been one to turn her back on any experience.

"Come back to me," he told her, and she realized it was Luc. Luc Benoit, with origins at least as humble as her own and the same ability to rise above them. He didn't belong here, but she could feel him leaning over her, tears streaming down the broad planes of his cheeks as he called to her.

"It's an illusion," Esther warned. She held out her hand, reaching out from one world into the next, but Rebekah couldn't stop looking at Luc. He believed in her. He *wanted* her. After a thousand years of life she was still a woman who could be loved and admired and needed. All she had to do was keep living.

Rebekah hesitated for a moment that stretched out into eternity, torn between two desires so powerful that either one of them could consume her whole. She couldn't bring herself to choose, and her indecision was enough to break the connection to the Other Side. Esther gave a gasping sigh, and the shimmering in the air hardened and then vanished.

"Mother!" Rebekah screamed, but it was too late: Her doubt had done its work. The Other Side closed itself to her, then the sunlight faltered and winked out. Rebekah swallowed hard, tasting bitter disappointment as the world of her childhood melted away. She should have known that her mother wouldn't hold out her hand forever. Esther wasn't the type of parent who rewarded cowardice.

"I still belong here, then," Rebekah told the waiting darkness, letting it surround her and seep into her skin. "I want to live."

It was true, she realized. She wanted life so desperately and suddenly that it took her breath away. Stars swarmed before her eyes and then tree branches made stripes of blackness against the sky. Luc's beautiful face stared anxiously into hers, and the cold, hard ground pressed into her spine.

"You came back!" Luc exclaimed, kissing her passionately on the mouth.

Rebekah pushed him away, her body still trying to remember how to breathe. She sucked in air once and then again, feeling the strange way it whistled around the hole in her chest. "You tried to kill me," she gasped when she was able to speak, and she touched the ragged edges of her wound gingerly. "You *did* kill me."

The stake was in his hand. Rebekah understood that he must have pulled it from her heart—he had just saved her from dying. But the sight of it chilled her, and for a moment it was as if time might run backward as easily as forward. Rebekah couldn't tear her eyes away from the broken branch in Luc's hand.

The tree spread above them, its leaves rustling ever so slightly in the first breezes of the morning. The eastern sky was light, Rebekah realized, and the faint, pinkish glow of dawn warmed Luc's blond hair. His gaze followed hers, and he dropped the stake as if it had burned his skin.

"I would never hurt you," he swore. "That man did something to me, the powder he had . . . I don't know, exactly. I had no choice in what I did."

"You called to me," Rebekah said, feeling the muscles above her heart beginning to repair. "Did Tomás force you to bring me back?"

"No," Luc answered, his voice loaded with conviction. "It felt like a fog was lifting, and then I saw you." He hesitated, struggling to find the right words. "I saw you *before*. Lying here with my stake in your chest, but also running through the forest with your brothers. There was a cottage . . . you were everywhere around me, living here as a human."

"I saw all of that, too." Rebekah pulled herself up to a seated position, her fingertips exploring the hole. There had been so many wounds over the years, yet none of them had left a visible scar. To anyone who saw her, she might still be that girl who had played beneath this tree with flowers in her hair. Only she knew otherwise.

"I could feel your love," Luc told her. "I could feel your will to live, and how much this world meant to you. That's what saved you, Rebekah; that's what let me call you back. You have the most powerful heart of anyone I have ever met, and your heart is what saved you."

"This time," she muttered, watching her skin slowly close over the hole the stake had left. She reached for the stake, feeling the ache of the wound as she moved. The stake was too valuable to leave behind, even if Tomás's attack had changed everything. Rebekah might have come to Mystic Falls seeking revenge, but she had found far, far more than that.

"The sun is rising," she reminded Luc, and he looked east as if he had never seen a sunrise before.

"There's still time," Luc said, squinting at the

lightening sky. "Take all the time you need, Rebekah.... I will stay by your side."

"There's no need to stay here." Rebekah smiled, threading her arm through his. "Let's find some shelter for the day. We have plans to make, and more enemies than we need right now."

Rebekah and Luc walked arm in arm toward the little town, and Rebekah tucked the White Oak stake carefully into the inner pocket of her cloak.

TWELVE

"It's all right," Alejandra murmured, brushing one smooth hand along the side of Elijah's face while staring into his eyes. "Whatever you saw at the brothel, it doesn't have to matter."

He opened his mouth to argue, to explain why Klaus's betrayal had cut him so deeply, but he realized he didn't need to. Alejandra wasn't dismissing his outrage. She was showing him a way out.

With Alejandra by his side, Elijah wanted to find a way of enjoying his life that had nothing to do with power struggles. Klaus could have New Orleans and the pit of snakes it had become. If he wanted control of the city so badly, he was welcome to it.

"I always believed that staying together as a family was what made us strong," Elijah said at last, turning his head to kiss Alejandra's fingertips.

"But not anymore," Alejandra finished, withdrawing her hand gently to pick up a goblet of wine that sat on the table beside her.

"I allowed my siblings to lean on that strength like a crutch," Elijah went on, taking the goblet when she offered it. "I never understood how they could be so ungrateful, or how they could accuse me of holding them back when all I ever did was keep them safe. I should have allowed them to outgrow that protection; I've done them no favors by sheltering them. And it seems that they have thought so for quite some time."

"Drink," Alejandra urged, tipping the goblet toward him gently. "The past is over and done with, and it's more enjoyable to discuss our future."

"And for that you would prefer me drunk?" he teased, but he drained the goblet in one long swallow. The spiced wine seared his throat all the way down into his belly, and then its comforting heat began to seep out into Elijah's limbs. It had been a trying night, but he was already beginning to feel steadier, more sure. Just being with Alejandra seemed to make more sense than everything else in the last seventy years. He buried his head deeper into her lap.

"You feel better now," she guessed, her green eyes glittering in the sunlight that streamed through the windows of their hideaway. The house's late owner had had lavish tastes, and Elijah thought the silks and velvets that upholstered his great room were a particularly fitting backdrop for Alejandra's exotic beauty.

"I feel better now," he agreed.

Alejandra smiled and stretched, her shoulders rippling like a cat's after sleep. She had bathed and dressed while he had been gone, but Elijah could still remember every curve of the naked body beneath her gown. "You are a king wherever you go, my darling; I just want to come with you." She took the goblet from his unresisting hand, glancing into its empty depths with an unreadable smile.

"I wouldn't let you leave my side," Elijah whispered, reaching up to twist his fingers through her black curls. "You've opened my eyes. Your passion, your humanity. The freedom in which you live your life has inspired me to change my own. Whatever comes next is something I want to share only with you."

Alejandra smiled again, setting the goblet aside and leaning down to kiss him. "I think some time away from all this is exactly what we need," she suggested. "I know a place. You're too well known to steal away in daylight, but we can leave after night falls."

"How will we pass the time until then?" he asked, sitting up so that they were face-to-face on the daybed. He could think of several ways, and he could tell from the way Alejandra kissed him again that she had a few of the same ideas.

He savored the taste of her. She was far sweeter than the wine. As she climbed onto his lap he caught her by the waist and lifted her. Alejandra's legs twined around his torso, and Elijah felt a surge of desire so powerful he couldn't wait another moment. He spun around and pressed her back against the nearest wall, pushing her skirts aside.

He made short work of the clothing that separated them, and she gasped in pleasure as he entered her. She clung to him even more tightly as he began to move in her, each thrust pressing her more firmly against the wall behind her.

Elijah felt almost light-headed with anticipation. Alejandra smiled up at him, and the sheer joy of being with her nearly overwhelmed him.

"The boat is just ahead," she promised, guiding him along the edge of the bayou by some process of navigation too convoluted for him to follow at the moment.

"You have a boat waiting?" Elijah asked, amused. They had spent every moment together since he had agreed to leave the city earlier that day, and he knew she hadn't sent word ahead during that time. She had been otherwise engaged. "You must have been very confident that I would agree to come with you."

Alejandra's smile grew sly. "Don't you remember how we met?" she teased. "I can tell the future, and as soon as I took your hand I knew all sorts of things about what would happen between us."

Elijah laughed, hearing a new openness in the sound. When was the last time he had really laughed? "I should never bet against you, then, my love. I'll try to remember."

"That won't be a problem," Alejandra assured him smugly. "According to your palm, we will always be on the same side from now on."

The whole city could burn down, for all he cared. All he wanted was his fortune-teller, her dark curls and warm limbs, and the freedom she had showed him. He could go wherever he wanted, do whatever he wanted, spend a year making love to Alejandra without giving a second thought to what else might be going on in the world.

The boat was waiting by the edge of a narrow river that disappeared into a swamp. "Where will this lead?" Elijah asked curiously, trying to use the stars to determine whether its current ran toward the sea or the Mississippi River, but the constellations seemed to have moved to different parts of the sky.

"You'll see when we get there. For once, you aren't in control," Alejandra purred, and she rested the palm of her hand on his back. The warmth of it steadied him, bringing him back to earth and fixing the stars back into their proper places.

"I can agree to that . . . just this once," Elijah teased. He took the little canvas pack she carried and tossed it aboard, then swung Alejandra lightly onto the deck before jumping up after her. It was a small, shallow-bottomed craft, meant for the bayou and nothing else as far as he could tell. The boat had a surprisingly skillful carving at its prowl. It was a head with two faces, each profile facing in opposite directions. Four oarsmen waited for them, and stared at the deck when Alejandra was near, deferring to her as if she were some magnificent empress.

"Cast off," she ordered, and they obeyed. Elijah could understand how they must feel—he was also dizzy when she was near. And to think that he had been ready to settle with a chain around his neck and Lisette at his right hand . . . Lisette, who had turned on him so quickly.

The memory of her sitting beside Klaus was painful and yet distant. It was almost as if years had passed since then, instead of only a few hours. Elijah was so sure of his new course, so committed to his new life, that the old one had already fallen away.

"I don't know that I've ever come out this way before," he remarked, squinting again at the stars. They seemed to move when he wasn't looking, playing some children's game to confuse him. The landmarks around the boat were also strange to him. Not even someone who lived forever could memorize the miles of bayou that spread around New Orleans.

But Alejandra knew their direction, standing on the deck like Cleopatra at the head of her navy. "You would have no reason to visit these parts," she assured him, and Elijah wondered what sort of business had brought her here before. It seemed strange, but the whole world seemed mysterious to him at the moment.

They rode together for what felt like hours, the only sound the gentle lapping of the water against the boat's wooden hull. An oarsman shouted, and the boat slowed. Elijah's keen eyesight could just barely make out a few straight lines out in front of them. It was a low, vine-covered cabin with a thatched roof, a humble dwelling that was miles away from its closest neighbor.

"How did you ever find this place?" he asked in amazement, peering doubtfully at the cabin. It could not have had more than one small room, and from where he stood it looked cold and empty. He couldn't imagine Alejandra in such a place, although he himself had lived in worse from time to time, when the situation had called for it.

"I have many secrets," she reminded him, and the boat bumped up against the shore beside the cabin.

Elijah jumped down, soaking his boots in the shallows of the tiny river, and then held his arms up for Alejandra. For a moment, as his hands circled her waist, his head swam with the memory of the way they had spent their morning together.

Alejandra let him lift her down onto slightly more solid ground, although the surrounding swamp still sucked at their feet as they made their way toward the little cabin. Behind him, the men began unloading crates of supplies. Elijah was impressed with Alejandra's planning. With only part of a day in which to prepare, she really had thought of everything.

A crocodile watched them from the tall grass, its tail swaying back and forth with a movement that reminded Elijah of a cat's. "Shoo," Alejandra told it coolly, waving a dismissive hand in its direction. The beast's black eyes flashed, then it sunk back into the swamp. "Mind the vines," she added to Elijah, shoving the cabin's door open on its rusted hinges.

He could tell instantly that this had once been

her home. Alejandra had never spoken much of her upbringing, but he had somehow imagined her as a black sheep—the sensual, free-spirited, mystical outcast of a genteel, middle-class family. Now, though, he wasn't so sure.

As he held open the door for her, his left hand brushed against one of the vines that nearly swallowed the doorframe. It stung and then burned, and Elijah frowned in surprise to see welts rising on his skin. The pain was mild, yet it made his head swim and the cabin blur and slide.

Then the sensation was gone, and Elijah focused on Alejandra's concerned green eyes, the furrow of worry between her eyebrows. "Come inside," she urged him. "This place has many untamed dangers."

It was cold and unwelcoming in the cabin, but Elijah built a fire while Alejandra hung lanterns. Soon it was almost cozy, although it was even smaller and shabbier than he had guessed from the outside. A thin, faded patchwork quilt covered the sagging bed, and the rest of the space was taken up with a table and chairs beside the low hearth. The air was stale and musty, but the fire crackled merrily, and the smoke was sweet.

"Welcome to our little hideaway," Alejandra murmured, pulling him toward the bed, and Elijah forgot everything else in the heat of her touch.

THIRTEEN

*H*eaps of dead bodies covered the floor of the Mikaelsons' mansion. Klaus paced among them, stalking from one room to the next and pausing occasionally to look out the windows for the first signs of the rising moon.

"Why aren't they waking?" Sampson demanded, prowling around the bodies as if his anger could hurry the magic along.

"Patience," Klaus muttered, and the werewolf snorted at the rather obvious irony. "It will happen any minute now."

But Klaus could feel his victory slipping out of his hands.

"Lisette!" he shouted, and she looked up from her place beside one of the corpses. "How long until moonrise?"

"Now." She shrugged. "Now, or in a minute, but I would have expected—"

One of the dead bodies stirred and shivered, and every single conscious person in the room turned toward it. The prisoner gave a rattling cough, and Klaus noticed that the front of his rough-spun shirt was saturated with dried blood.

"The ones in the hall are also moving," a werewolf with long red hair called out, and Klaus saw more of the corpses beginning to twitch.

"Finally," Sampson growled. "That human cult's ranks are swelling every day, from the sound of it."

"We'll have no trouble putting down their rebellion now," Klaus replied. The first prisoner coughed again, and Klaus approached him. "They just need to drink human blood to fully transform." There was plenty of that in the mansion—they were ready.

"Never," a hoarse voice gasped, and Klaus glared in surprise at the bloodstained man at his feet. The convict's eyes were open at last. He took in the bodies around him and the vampire standing over him. "We will never turn against our own."

"You are no longer human," Lisette corrected, her

tone leaving no room for compromise. "You've already turned against what you were."

The man lifted his hands, patting at his hips and chest as if to make sure his body was still there. Then he raised them to his face. His Adam's apple bobbed in his throat as he swallowed hard. "You're wrong," he replied. "I won't."

His body was wracked with sudden spasms, and Klaus leapt to his side. All around them the other prisoners were shifting, stretching, and testing their limbs, but Klaus didn't trust what was happening.

"What's wrong with you?" he demanded, pulling the prisoner's hands away from his face. There was a tiny glass vial clasped between his fingers with one end bitten off—the glass jagged, the vessel empty.

Klaus grabbed it and cautiously tasted the liquid. He cursed as it touched his lips. "Werewolf venom," he snarled. He was half werewolf and immune to its poison, but any other vampire who drank it would die. A new vampire didn't stand a chance against its poison.

"They all have it!" Lisette shouted from another corner of the room. She crossed over the bodies quickly, hurrying to get close to Klaus. "Your blood," she whispered, so low that even he could barely hear her at first. "Couldn't it—? Couldn't you—?"

"Perhaps that's what *they* want," Klaus reasoned,

keeping a wary eye on Sampson. It was true that his unique blood would counteract the poison, but half the convicts were too far gone to save. "Maybe the Collados hope that I'll weaken myself to save the new vampires, and then they'll turn on me when I can't protect myself." The idea lodged itself in his mind, taking on new significance.

Klaus stood and rounded on Sampson, who was prying a broken vial out of another man's hand. "What treachery is this?" Klaus demanded, grabbing the burly wolf by the collar. "What game do you think you're playing?"

Sampson shoved Klaus away and straightened his coat. "You think I let you kill hundreds of men just for the pleasure of watching them die a second time?" he asked. "I'm not as much of a monster as you are, Klaus."

A little trickle of froth ran from the prisoner's mouth, and his eyes stayed fixed on the ceiling. They would all die, Klaus realized. All their work would be for nothing.

"We didn't plan any of this," the red-haired werewolf insisted, kicking a newly dead prisoner in her frustration. "Don't be absurd."

"It's just a coincidence, then, that it's your toxin they all carry?" Klaus pulled a vial from a third man and held it up to emphasize his point. "How many of the citizens of New Orleans have one of these hidden on them tonight?"

"How the hell should I know?" Sampson's face reddened a bit in his outrage.

"You *should* know," Lisette pointed out, closing the eyes of one of the prisoners. "You knew that humans were arming themselves with supernatural weapons, yet you continued to turn a profit off the weapon your own bodies make. Did it ever occur to you that this armed, organized cult would take advantage of that?"

"We don't sell our venom here," Sampson said stiffly, then he tasted the glass vial in his hand. "Wherever they got this, it wasn't from us."

"Wherever they got it," Klaus repeated, tossing his vial aside and beginning to pace again. The men were dying in earnest now, but there were no screams or even groans of pain. It was a suicide pact, and they were all in it to the last. "You send your poison up the river to sell it there, and your friends upriver send theirs down here. Your hands are always clean, yet somehow your filth spreads everywhere."

"I'd heard you were paranoid, but this is absurd," Sampson snapped. "You make it sound like we came to you, revealed the spy in your midst, and allied with you just to play some schoolboy prank. What could we possibly stand to gain by all of this?"

"What did *I* gain?" Klaus shouted. Rebekah had run off and Elijah had made his dramatic exit, and there was no one to hold Klaus back. And yet his plan had still been foiled, as if he were always predestined to fail.

The guard had warned him, he realized, back when they had first stormed the prison. He had said that Klaus would get nothing from the humans there except for blood. He had known . . . they had all known. The entire city was rising up against the vampires, and now Klaus couldn't even make new ones. Any he managed to turn would just find another way to die.

"They won't fight for us," Lisette murmured, and Klaus knew that she had arrived at the same conclusion. "Even without the venom, they were never going to join our cause. This was pointless from the start."

Sampson glared at her, then back at Klaus. Surrounded by the magnificent setting of the mansion, the wolf looked especially crude and out of place. To Klaus it seemed like a stray dog had snuck in off the street and was shedding its filthy fur all over the Turkish silk carpet, and he suddenly wished Rebekah were there to throw the mongrel out.

Where the hell was she, anyway? It wasn't like Klaus's siblings to leave him to his own devices for this long.

"Get out," Klaus snapped. "This isn't a matter that

requires your cooperation, so I invite you and your pack to get the hell out of my house right now."

Sampson looked as though he intended to argue, then seemed to think the better of it. He was too timid a leader to truly ally with, Klaus decided. He was more in Elijah's mold, always considering politics and angles rather than trusting his instincts.

"Have it your way." Sampson shrugged. "We won't be much help with this sort of situation, anyway. We've never experienced such a colossal failure—not until we teamed up with you." The werewolf turned and left, abandoning him just like Elijah and Rebekah had. No wonder he had so little faith in anyone but himself: He was the only person he could rely on.

"What the hell are we going to do with all these bodies?" Klaus complained when the last werewolf had left. He knelt and tugged one of the dead men's eyelids open.

"Well, it's not as if they're coming back," Lisette said, pushing a corpse out of the way so she could lounge on a velvet settee. "But the werewolves will, once they've calmed down and thought things through. We can't just leave these men lying around."

"True," Klaus agreed, watching a man spasm beside the marble fireplace. "If any of them do manage to rise, they will be enemies."

Lisette stared at the corpse she had just moved aside. "You want us to . . . to make sure they stay dead," she sighed.

"It's what they wanted. And we can't refuse a dead man's last wishes," Klaus replied sarcastically. As irritating as he sometimes found Lisette, she had stayed. There weren't many people in Klaus's life who could say the same, especially not at the moment. Cold moonlight streamed through the windows, washing the corpses in sickly white.

"Stake them all," Klaus ordered, raising his voice to carry throughout the mansion, so that everyone could hear him. "Make sure every convict stays dead."

It was gruesome, boring, thankless work. Most of the prisoners had died already, but others thrashed and struggled when the vampires approached with their stakes in hand. Even with their last breaths the convicts seemed determined to make things as difficult as possible.

Even worse, Klaus's army had begun their task in a disorganized, haphazard way, leaving some un-staked corpses littered between the ones who had already been put out of their misery. Hands twitched up to catch at Klaus's ankles when he least expected it, and he caught himself re-staking at least a few of the men.

"We're going at this all wrong," Lisette complained,

echoing Klaus's own irritated thoughts. "They should have been ordered to move the staked ones outside from the start."

"How nice to hear about one more thing I've done wrong," Klaus snapped, regretting his earlier moments of sympathy toward her. "If you don't like your orders, love, you can always go running after my brother. Maybe this time he'll tolerate your company. Better him than me."

Lisette straightened from the convict she had been crouched over, shoving her hair away from her face with a rough, angry thrust of her hand. "You keep worrying at that old bone, Klaus. It makes me wonder what your obsession is with Elijah's romantic life. Do you really live so much in his shadow that when you see me all you can think of is him?"

"What else should I think of?" Klaus hissed, stung in spite of himself. "Your lack of discipline or dedication to my cause? Your incompetence? Let's not forget whose brilliant idea this massacre was in the first place."

"It *was* a brilliant plan!" Lisette shouted, forgetting any pretense at composure. "You thought so, too, before you went and ran your mouth about it to anyone who would listen. Did you forget that these humans have been spying on you, manipulating you, and generally leading you around by the nose for weeks already? Did you think they would just sit on their hands and let you turn their soldiers into yours?"

Klaus was blinded by his own rage, and when his vision cleared he found that he had shoved the impertinent brat against the wall, his forearm pressed against her throat. "I don't see you living to eternity with a mouth like that," he seethed, his voice low and menacing. He realized that he still held a wooden stake in his free hand, and he touched the deadly point to Lisette's lightly freckled chest.

"Maybe you're right, if I have to deal with you forever," she spat, more angry than afraid, even with a stake poised right above her heart.

He drew the stake back, ready to drive it straight through her ribs, when a commotion by the front door forced him to hesitate.

"What the hell have you done?" a familiar voice shrieked, climbing into registers that were actually painful to Klaus's ears. "Pack up this butchery immediately and get it out of my house."

Klaus released Lisette, his moment of rage over. "It's my house, too," he shouted, stepping across a drawing room's worth of corpses to confront Rebekah in the hall. "You ran away again, so I've been managing things in your absence, dearest sister."

He expected her to have some kind of snappish

retort, but Rebekah's blue eyes blazed with unexpected rage the moment they met his, and Klaus was entirely unprepared for the immediate fury of her attack.

"You've terrorized this family for long enough, you son of a bitch," Rebekah snarled, her pretty face twisted into a mask of absolute loathing. She had a stake of her own, Klaus realized, and then he gave it a better look. He hadn't seen the wood of the White Oak tree in centuries, but he would know it anywhere.

At long last, Rebekah had made up her mind to kill him.

FOURTEEN

Rebekah's anger had taken on a real, tangible life of its own. Her return journey from Mystic Falls had been consumed by vengeful thoughts of Tomás, but when she walked in her front door and saw Klaus with a stake pressed to Lisette's heart, Rebekah's old pain had all flooded back.

Rebekah had lost a great deal over the centuries, and sometimes she believed she was used to it. But then some new, fresh hurt, like the murder of Marguerite Leroux, would remind her that her heart wasn't entirely scarred over. She couldn't let Klaus take one more person from her, and she couldn't possibly fight Tomás with a traitor hovering behind her back.

She pulled the stake from her cloak and flew at Klaus. Her brother blocked it, but clearly recognized that she meant to hurt him. All the other vampires fled from the room—they knew better than to get between a Mikaelson and a Mikaelson.

"You've gone too far," she told him. "Enough is enough. You destroy everything you touch."

"Is this about your precious carpets?" Klaus demanded. He made a grab for the stake, but she had no intention of handing it over. "It's hardly the first time they've seen a bit of blood. It comes out one way or another."

"You monster!" Rebekah shouted. "Have you forgotten what you did already? Do you ruin lives so easily that you can't even keep track of them all anymore?"

"I don't know what the hell you're talking about," Klaus snapped, watching the stake warily. "Put that thing down, or I'll kill you with it before you get the chance to threaten me again."

"You killed my friend, and Lisette was next!" Rebekah cried, holding her ground. She raised the stake again, but her hand quavered.

"I've killed lots of people's friends," Klaus replied, unimpressed by her anger. "It never seemed to be a problem before. Rebekah, put the stake down."

"You killed her *because* she was my friend." Rebekah could see a spark of curiosity on Klaus's face as her accusation penetrated his thick skull. Perhaps he had finally remembered the lengths he had gone to just to murder an innocent girl. "Marguerite never did anything to you, but you just had to get back at me, didn't you? And to put her in my bed! You staked a *child* to hurt me, Niklaus."

"Marguerite?" Klaus asked, as if he honestly didn't know what she was talking about. "That stray witch you took in a couple of decades back? I don't think I've seen her all week, dear sister." He paused and then frowned. "She's dead?"

"Don't toy with me," Rebekah warned, clenching her fist around the stake. She hated to think he was playing dumb to trick her; it was beneath them both.

"I didn't kill her, Rebekah." Klaus shrugged, as if the topic truly bored him. "Not after the first time, anyway. Not since you made her a vampire. I have no idea what happened to her, dead or alive. I've been a bit busy, as you can see."

Rebekah glanced down at the floor in spite of herself, taking in the dozens of dead bodies that filled their mansion. "I see you're up to your usual madness," she replied. "You really think I'll take this bloodbath as proof that you *didn't* kill the one person I actually cared about?"

"I don't have to prove anything to you." Klaus held up his hands to signal a truce. "If I killed someone to send a message to you, it would make no sense to deny it now. And here I am, dear sister, denying it."

You are going to lose everything you love, Rebekah, Tomás's voice echoed in her mind. *I know what you are afraid of. This is only the beginning.*

Rebekah heard the White Oak stake clatter to the marble floor. Tomás had taunted her, giving her the pieces of the puzzle but knowing she missed the essential key. "We're being used," she whispered, trying to force the whole picture to take shape. "I met a human, Niklaus, and he said things that . . . I think he's trying to drive us apart."

"A human?" Klaus asked sharply, picking up the stake from the floor. He looked for a moment as if he might slide it into a pocket of his own, but Rebekah glared at him. Their truce was still fragile. As a compromise, Klaus opened a wrought-iron chest that stood against one wall, locked the stake inside, then held up his hands to show that they were empty. "The humans have been giving me some trouble as well. A group of rebels played me against the werewolves for weeks. Is that the sort of thing your human would do?"

"The werewolves?" Rebekah frowned. "Who would even *need* to turn you against the Collado pack? I didn't know that you could hate them even more than you already do."

"An outside observer might say the same about the two of us," Klaus pointed out reasonably. "But these humans aren't just trying to ruin friendships and spoil our happiness, dear sister. They mean business. They want us dead, so they're driving wedges into cracks, hoping we'll give in to our anger and mistrust. The problem is, it's working."

The news was a surprise, but it certainly tracked with what Rebekah had seen of Tomás. He'd forced Luc to attack Rebekah, but it had been much simpler to turn her against Klaus. It had only taken one well-executed murder, with the timing and the staging carefully planned. Tomás had killed Marguerite because Klaus had threatened her, and because Rebekah would believe that her brother had finally made good on those threats.

You are going to lose everything you love.

Rebekah was supposed to die in Mystic Falls, but if she escaped, Tomás had planned for her to return and kill Klaus—or for him to kill her in retaliation. A White Oak stake was a dangerous weapon, even for its wielder. Tomás didn't care which of them died first, because he intended to kill them all. Even if Rebekah had failed to follow through, Tomás was lining up werewolves to take her brother out. He had so many plans intersecting at once that he didn't even need to call on Klaus's old hatred for New Orleans's witches, although Rebekah was confident that they would not be forgotten.

"Is all this"—she gestured at the carnage on the floor—"the werewolves' work, then?"

Klaus smiled bitterly at the bodies that lay everywhere around them. "In some ways, but no. This was the work of the rebels. Their cult has gained more ground than I would ever have believed. Sampson Collado revealed to me that my human spy had become a double agent, and we agreed to work together to eliminate the human threat. The sabotage you see here was supposed to undermine our alliance."

"Your *alliance*?" Rebekah said, genuinely stunned. "You can't be serious." Either she had been away longer than she realized—lifetimes, perhaps—or Klaus was taking this human menace very, very seriously indeed. How had Elijah let this happen? And where was he, anyway? Surely he was aware of the human threat in their midst. He derived his deepest pleasures from such intricate plots.

"Where is Elijah?" she asked Klaus. Klaus looked guilty, or at least as guilty as he was capable of. "Oh, no. What did you do?" Rebekah demanded as a wave of foreboding washed over her. If Tomás had already turned Klaus and Elijah against each other . . .

"Elijah has abandoned us," Klaus announced, although his tone indicated that there was more to it than that. "I suspect it has something to do with the woman he's taken up with, honestly, although he burst in on me and Sampson Collado and picked a nasty fight all on his own."

Rebekah heard a sharp intake of breath from the drawing room, and she caught a glimpse of Lisette's reddish hair at the edge of the doorway.

"What woman?" Rebekah asked, lowering her voice in an attempt to be discreet. "Another vampire, you mean?"

"No, some two-bit fortune-teller who was hired on at my brothel." Klaus showed none of Rebekah's restraint, and his voice seemed to echo off the very walls. "Not even a real witch, just a . . ."

He trailed off and stared at Rebekah, who returned his panicked look. "A human?" she asked, her heart beating hard. "Elijah's been bedding some human woman, and then he fought with you, and now he's gone?"

Klaus nodded slowly.

"We have to find him," she said. "We have to find Elijah right now."

FIFTEEN

Elijah couldn't remember the last time he had been ill. He didn't think vampires *could* get sick. He had been poisoned, bewitched, and haunted, but as far as he could remember, he had never been sick.

He lay on top of the faded patchwork quilt, straining his eyes in order to see Alejandra make another concoction over the little hearth. She had spent days brewing strangely thin soups and foul-tasting teas, growing ever more creative as Elijah's sickness stubbornly refused leave. If anything, it only seemed to get worse.

The cabin's small room spun gently whenever Alejandra moved, and Elijah wondered if this was what seasickness felt like. He had only been on a ship once as a human, when his family had fled Europe to escape the plague. That voyage hadn't affected him, but he could still remember some of the other passengers looking just as nauseous and unsteady as he currently felt.

Alejandra bent to touch Elijah's forehead, and he shivered. "Is it even worse?" she asked, her voice filled with concern and sympathy. "I wish I could do more to help you."

"You're doing all that anyone could," Elijah said. He felt as if his very soul was being leached away, as if his mental strength was draining out of him along with the physical. He'd already lost track of the days and nights that had passed since their arrival—three at least, but it could just as easily have been a week.

It troubled him that no one would worry about his unexplained absence. It seemed like a particularly unfortunate coincidence that he had fallen ill at the same time he had cut himself off from his family. As he lay there, shivering and sweating in some shack in the middle of nowhere, it was impossible for Elijah to shake the feeling that the loss of his siblings was somehow linked to his illness.

"I need to warn them," Elijah reasoned, forgetting that he hadn't spoken aloud. Alejandra cocked her head curiously, and he wondered if she had grown used to his feverish madness.

"Warn whom?" she asked, and then draped another cool, damp cloth across Elijah's forehead. It smelled faintly medicinal, as if it had been steeped with herbs. She was trying, he knew, but no matter how much occult knowledge she may have stumbled across, Alejandra was clearly out of her depth.

"Rebekah," Elijah sighed, unwilling to name Klaus. It would make him seem weak—weaker—to admit that he was worried about the health of the brother who had so recently betrayed him. But old habits died hard, and Elijah had been looking out for Klaus his entire life.

"You don't know where Rebekah is," Alejandra told him gently, patiently, as if speaking to a child. She unbuttoned his shirt and ran an idle finger along his chest, pausing over the spot where she could feel his heartbeat. Her touch was clinical, offering none of its usual invitation. "Rebekah left New Orleans before you did, don't you remember that? She has always wanted to go off on her own and live the life that was taken from her, and she finally did it."

"She did?" Elijah asked. Alejandra's words conjured up images he wasn't sure he'd actually seen. Had he watched Rebekah ride out? Had they spoken; had she asked him to let her go? He could remember all of that now, even though he was positive it had never happened.

"Yes . . . we've been over this, Elijah." Alejandra sighed, examining his eyes closely. "Can you stand? If you wanted to, I mean, could you?"

"Of course," Elijah replied, stung by the question. "I could fight dragons for you, my love."

"That's not true, either." Alejandra laid two cool fingers along the side of Elijah's neck, remaining still for a few moments while his pulse beat erratically. "Did you know I grew up in this swamp? There was nowhere else for us to live after our father was killed, and our mother could barely take care of us."

Her voice was far away, almost dreamy. Elijah felt as though he were drifting downward, farther and farther from her lovely face. "'Us?'" he repeated, hearing a curious slackness in his voice. "You told me once that you didn't have siblings."

"We were terribly poor—my mother had come to the New World as an indentured servant, and spent every moment working," Alejandra continued, as if she hadn't heard him. "We had to fend for ourselves out here, to use whatever we could find in the bayou to survive."

"Did I know all this before?" Elijah asked, trying

to remember exactly what she had said about her life, and when. Perhaps Elijah had known about her upbringing all along, and had forgotten it in the haze of his illness. Now it was easy to imagine Alejandra as a child here. He could see her face round with youth and her black hair twisted into two thick plaits as she picked her way across the bayou with her brother, Klaus.

That was wrong, though. Klaus was *his* brother, and Alejandra had told Elijah that she had no siblings. He was sure of that, although he couldn't remember the precise words, or when he had heard them.

"You said . . ." Elijah paused, trying to remember exactly what she *had* said, and found himself unable to go on.

"*Shh, shh,* don't talk, my love." She smoothed the hair on his forehead and he relaxed into her touch. "It'll only confuse you more," she went on. "But I have thought of something that might cure you. There's a root that grows nearby. We used to make it into a tea for all sorts of unknown ailments. It's worth a try, my dearest."

Alejandra threw her cloak around her shoulders, then leaned over to kiss him on the cheek. She smelled like smoke and incense. "I'll be back before you know it," she promised.

He didn't want her to go, but he couldn't force his mouth open. She smiled and put a finger to his lips.

The door banged shut behind her, and Elijah stared at the low ceiling. It swayed, and he tried to count its movements like seconds. He wondered if Alejandra had been right—was he already too weak to stand?

Elijah swung his legs over the edge of the thin mattress and dragged his torso upright. He had definitely been overly optimistic when he had said he could fight, but he'd be damned if some mystery illness would keep him off his feet entirely.

It was the hardest thing he'd ever done, but Elijah slowly forced his body upright. The room spun dangerously, but he refused to succumb to his mind's tricks. He stood, and after a few minutes he convinced himself to take a few halting, unsteady steps.

He felt as though he had been in a fog ever since he'd met Alejandra. It had been a beautiful, delirious haze, and he thought it was love. But now that same fog had taken over his mind and body, and Elijah couldn't see his way out. It scared him.

The strangest part was that Elijah *still* loved her, even as doubts swirled in his mind. The thought of being at odds with her was almost physically painful. All he wanted was to be persuaded that he was wrong, that his suspicions were nothing but mere hallucinations.

That, more than anything else, convinced Elijah that something was terribly wrong with him.

The pack Alejandra had brought with her was just a few short steps away, but his vision stretched so that it looked like miles. Alejandra would be back soon—he had to hurry.

Elijah dragged his left foot forward, then shifted his weight and worked to move his right. Every few seconds, he thought he could hear footsteps approaching outside, and he had to force himself to concentrate on his goal. He couldn't spare the energy to take a few extra steps and look out the tiny window.

Elijah collapsed with a sigh of relief when he finally reached the bag. Fumbling with the clasps took nearly all the strength and dexterity he had left, but he had come too far to give up now. The pack contained a few simple dresses, a comb made of horn, a tiny jar of some kind of sweet-smelling cream. Elijah pawed awkwardly through all the usual things a woman might bring on a journey until his numbed fingers bumped up against a small paper envelope that didn't belong.

He tore it a bit as he opened it, cursing his weak-limbed clumsiness, but when he saw the powder inside he forgot everything else. He had never seen it before, but he knew it at once: Its curious, shining flecks were exactly what the legends had always described.

"So it seems you *were* able to stand," Alejandra remarked from the doorway. Elijah felt his blood turn to ice at the sound of her voice, afraid of the desire it aroused in him even now. She had laid her trap well, and he was thoroughly tangled in it. "Tell me, what have you found in there?"

Elijah felt compelled to turn, although his body protested at every movement. The powder she'd secretly been giving him had rendered him all but helpless. "Where did you get *vinaya* powder?" he asked, his tongue feeling thick and heavy in his mouth.

"We collect curiosities," explained the man who walked in after Alejandra, and behind him Elijah could see a dozen lanterns or more. He was trapped, hemmed in by humans and too weak to even think of overpowering them.

"Your kind has an unnatural advantage over us," Alejandra added, her voice cold and detached. "We had to even out the odds if we wanted to take back our city."

"Witches all over the coast practically begged to trade with us," the man went on. He was tall, with black hair that curled just to his shoulders. His body was shrouded in a thick black cloak with a glittering silver pin at its throat. "They relayed potions and weapons from all over the world, including some cuttings of the vine that makes that cunning little powder in your hand."

"Vinaya," Elijah repeated. He now recognized the vines that grew around the cabin—similar to poison ivy, glossy and red at the stem, but with a fourth leaf. A plant like that was supposed to be the main ingredient in vinaya powder. The story went that vinaya's creators believed vampires could be made human again, and vinaya powder was the horrible result of their good intentions. The witches' original enchantment had failed, but they'd unleashed a potent concoction that allowed a human to control any vampire who ingested it. Any trace of the spell had disappeared centuries ago and had never been heard of again . . . until now. "You put it in the wine you gave me the day we left?"

"And in everything since then as well," Alejandra confirmed. "It takes time for the powder's strength to build up to a level that gives me permanent control. My twin here likes to use it for immediate effect, but I find his methods less reliable. With a vampire of your experience and power, I couldn't take any chance of the vinaya wearing off . . . and now I can promise you that it won't."

The tall man smiled fondly at Alejandra. "We each have our strengths, sister," he agreed, sounding almost playful. He wrapped his arm around her shoulders, and

Elijah was consumed by the desire to tear his throat out.

"Your twin?" Elijah asked, looking from her to the man and back again. There were similarities, now that he thought to look for them: The man had Alejandra's patrician nose and high, sharp cheekbones. His green eyes were a few shades lighter in color than hers, but they had the same languid, feline shape to them.

"Did I never mention him before?" she asked, smiling up at the man in a way Elijah recognized well. The cabin might be where Alejandra had lived as a child, but the man beside her was her home.

"My name is Tomás," the man said pleasantly, releasing Alejandra and taking a menacing step closer to Elijah. "You are Elijah Mikaelson, and you are going to help me and my sister destroy your brother, your sister, and then every last one of the vermin you three have created to infest our city."

Before Elijah could answer, Tomás lifted his hand to his mouth and blew onto his palm, scattering a fine, iridescent powder into Elijah's face. It burned, but he was too weak to cry out.

"You will have no choice," one of them gloated, but through the red haze that consumed him, Elijah could not have even said which twin had spoken.

SIXTEEN

Where the hell was Elijah?

Klaus prowled the floor as if a map to his brother's location might appear if he kept pacing. He had begun his search for Elijah in Alejandra's spare little room above the Southern Spot and now, days later, he had memorized the cracks in the floorboards.

There wasn't much in the room *aside* from its floorboards. Klaus didn't make it his business to pry into his employees' lives, but he wished he had noticed sooner that his fortune-teller didn't actually seem to live in the quarters she was assigned. The bed didn't look as though it had ever been slept in, and if

Alejandra had ever kept any personal effects there, she had taken them with her.

Klaus knew there was nothing useful in the empty room. But he didn't know where else to go, and giving up the search was not an option. Elijah must be counting on his siblings to find him, and they'd already lost too much time dealing with the Cult of Janus. It was bad enough to have been tricked, but now he was also helpless.

There had to be *something* that would lead them to Alejandra—and to Elijah, if they were even together. Klaus couldn't shake the fear that he might be running out of time.

"No one has been here in days, if ever," Rebekah sighed from the doorway. "Sampson and his pack have been moving west along the river, and you should be out there with them, Niklaus. The trail here is cold."

"Even a cold trail has to start somewhere," Klaus argued stubbornly, although he was debating his own doubts as much as his sister's. "We don't have any other leads."

"We do now," Lisette's freckled face appeared beside Rebekah's in the doorway. "The wolves found a track, but they lost it again. They think Alejandra and your brother boarded a boat at the edge of the bayou, but they have no way of narrowing down where they went from there."

The news gave Klaus a dim hope. He was a better tracker than any werewolf, or at least any werewolf stuck in its useless human form—his nose and eyesight were both far superior. Maybe the boat had left traces as it pushed through the swamp, signs that the wolves were too dense to pick up on. It was possible, but not quite enough to persuade him to give up on any other leads. "The vampires I sent to the warehouse district have turned up nothing?"

"Not yet," Lisette admitted. "If this Tomás really is masquerading as a merchant, then it's an excellent disguise. We haven't found anything down there that doesn't belong. I sent José on ahead to tell them about the boat, so they'll start looking for any that might have been out in the bayou recently."

"Go with José," Klaus ordered as Lisette gave him a pleading look. "Don't argue with me now. I need you to take charge of the hunt for the boat, so that my brother has our best people at every front of this search. He needs us all."

Lisette's lips went white as she pushed her mouth together in a grudging silence, then she turned and ran down the hallway without a word.

Klaus shoved the doors of the little wardrobe open again, trying to recall everything he had ever noticed of Alejandra's habits. He had never paid much attention to her, not even after learning of her dalliance with Elijah. He thought he knew everything he needed to, and hadn't bothered to seek out more gossip from the laundresses.

That thought gave him an idea so simple, so obvious, that Klaus was halfway out of the empty room before his mind had fully wrapped around his plan.

"Where are you going?" Rebekah shouted after him, but Klaus had already reached the back staircase, taking the steps three at a time in his hurry to reach the little courtyard behind the brothel where the washing was done.

"Hold where you are," he ordered, bursting into the courtyard so abruptly that a sturdy, apple-cheeked woman shrieked in alarm. Her calloused hands were submerged in soapy water.

"Sir!" she squeaked.

"Do you have anything that belongs to the fortune-teller?" he demanded, rifling through the nearest pile of flimsy, silky gowns. Alejandra hadn't worked in days, but the Southern Spot went through an impressive amount of clothing and bedding, and often nonessentials could pile up.

"I think that's one of her dresses hanging on the line there," a young maid suggested, pointing to a green linen gown. "It's almost dry, if she's able to wait until morning."

"She can wait," Klaus growled. "Is there anything of hers left to be cleaned?"

The women looked at each other nervously, and then the younger one pointed again. "With spring around the corner we've got a lot of outer-clothes no one seems to want right away," she explained, and Klaus saw a pile of cloaks pushed off to one side of the courtyard. "We haven't gotten to any of those ones there yet."

"That fortune-teller always has fancy embroidery and beading and such," the apple-cheeked woman added, seeming to have recovered her composure at last. "Hélène insists on doing that kind of thing herself, but she's been down with the flux all week." She stepped away from her work. "I'm sure there will be something there. I'll help you look."

Klaus knew Alejandra's cloak as soon as the laundress uncovered it. It was midnight-blue velvet, embroidered with tiny silver stars that danced into all kinds of fanciful constellations as the fabric moved. The collar was set with glass cut to look like gemstones, and there was a faint, familiar smell on it: the suggestion of the Southern

Spot permeating the rich folds. But after a moment Klaus was able to discern another layer: a smoky scent that could only belong to Alejandra herself.

"That's it," he announced shortly, ignoring the confused look the laundresses exchanged with each other. "You ladies have my undying gratitude," he added over his shoulder, as he caught Rebekah just coming off the staircase and spun her around toward the front door. "This way, dear sister," he told her. "I know what we're tracking now."

Boot prints crisscrossed the mud where the wolves had lost the trail. "Your wolves have made a mess of this," Klaus observed as Sampson joined him and Rebekah.

"We got this far." The muscular werewolf shrugged. "If you're able to carry on the search from here without us, we'll accept your heartfelt gratitude and fall back."

Rebekah laughed at the pack leader's brazenness, and Sampson flashed a grin at her before stepping away. The wolves were in high spirits as their leader called them off the hunt. They had cobbled together a crude but sturdy raft, and Klaus saw Rebekah usher the last of the werewolves away from it. She took one of the long oars for herself and pushed into the shallow water.

Klaus stepped into the slow river and cast about for any hint of Alejandra's scent. When he caught a trace of her perfume a dozen yards downstream, he pushed off to pursue it, waving vaguely to catch his sister's attention as he went.

Rebekah caught up to him after a few moments, steering her raft through the sluggish water. "Come aboard, and help me keep this thing on course," she ordered. "The wolves didn't build it with ease of navigation in mind, although I'll give them credit for keeping me out of that brackish mess you're floundering in."

Klaus hauled himself out of the sucking mud and crouched on the rough logs that made up the raft. "Head west for now," he said, "but there's no such thing as a steady bearing out here." The overgrown swamp was all twists and switchbacks, defying any ordinary attempt at navigation. But Klaus could almost see Alejandra's scent, beckoning him from deep in the bayou. Hours passed as Klaus and Rebekah floated down the river. He'd never been this deep into the marshes before— nothing good ever happened out here.

"It's gone," Klaus said suddenly. The faint trace of Alejandra had dissipated, and farther downstream there was nothing but the ordinary stench of the bayou.

Rebekah stuck her oar into the mud at the bottom of the river, then pushed them toward the muddy bank. "It must pick up there," she said, jerking her chin toward an opening along the bank. It was a big enough gap for a boat to let passengers ashore.

Klaus tested the air. He blocked out the bullfrogs and cicadas, attuning all his senses to the one person he had to find as they left the raft behind. Alejandra had come this way, he thought, but her trail was quickly overwhelmed by the smell of burning peat. Klaus heard the crackle of a fire and then the low chatter of voices nearby. "Stop," he hissed to Rebekah. "There are easily a dozen of them." He gestured for her to follow him.

The humans sat around a fire that was downwind of a little cabin, but Klaus could also smell the moonshine amid the smoke. They were well on the far side of drunk and hadn't even bothered to post sentries. A well-worn track of boot prints led from the fire to the cabin, and Klaus was almost positive he recognized Elijah's tread.

A hawk-nosed woman lifted a bottle in an impromptu toast to Janus, and the rest of the humans followed suit and cheered. Klaus felt the hair on the back of his neck stand up. What horrible thing had happened to inspire this festive mood? And what did it have to do with his brother?

Klaus longed to kill them all, but it was as if Elijah's voice was in his ear, reminding him to exercise restraint and plan out his steps.

"I'll take the six on the left," Rebekah offered, "and you can have the six on the right. Fair?"

Klaus gritted his teeth together and shook his head. "Let's get the lay of the land first," he said, barely recognizing himself.

He felt Rebekah's head snap toward him and could feel the shocked look on her face. He flicked his eyes toward his sister and gave her his most innocent smile. One of the humans split away from the group, and Klaus followed, moving through the tree cover. The man was fumbling with his trousers when Klaus caught him by the collar, wrapping a hand around his mouth in case he was a screamer. The man's eyes bulged with fear once he saw Klaus, but he didn't struggle. Klaus guessed his reputation had preceded him.

"You're not on my list at the moment," Klaus reassured him softly. "Let's keep it that way, shall we?"

The man nodded, his eyes wide.

"Good." Klaus smiled, moving his hand down from the man's mouth to grip his throat. "I'm looking to surprise a few friends of yours. I need you to tell me exactly where they are, and how well armed."

"One of them used some kind of witchcraft on me," Rebekah warned, approaching Klaus and his new friend from the other side of the campfire. "It was a powder that burned. What other tricks do your leaders have up their sleeves?"

"And what have they done with our brother?" Klaus growled, making sure the hostage understood the importance of the question.

The man swallowed, his Adam's apple rising and falling against the pressure of Klaus's hand. "You've come too late, vampires." He gasped. "Our lady Alejandra has already done her work on the abomination in the cabin, and he's no longer any brother of yours. He's one of us now, and he's going to deliver our city back into our hands, where it belongs."

"You could have just said 'He's in the cabin,'" Rebekah replied, moving away as Klaus snapped the man's neck with a twist of his hand. "Let's go."

As Klaus stalked past, shouts of alarm rose from the circle around the fire, but Klaus didn't want to waste his time with them. The only people who mattered were inside the cabin.

A woman grabbed a heavy staff and jumped in front of Klaus, shouting at him to stop.

"If you want to live, I suggest that you run. Now," Klaus said. Then he pried the staff from the woman's hands and struck her in the face, hard enough to shatter her cheekbone. She collapsed and clutched her bloody jaw, moaning with pain. "You won't get a better offer from me," Klaus announced to the rest of the humans.

A handful broke and ran, but a group held their ground, making a desperate stand between the vine-covered cabin and the two furious vampires. "You may be powerful, but we are many," warned a man. "Your kind thrives on darkness and secrecy, but you have been exposed, and that will be your undoing. You can't kill us all, and we will no longer bend to your will."

"We can't kill you all?" Rebekah asked, sounding amused. She lunged forward, lifted the man by his throat, and threw him against an oak tree. "Anyone who stands between me and my brother will learn otherwise."

Klaus saw another man reach for a pouch at his belt, but before he could warn Rebekah the man had withdrawn a handful of purple vervain flowers. He threw them squarely in Rebekah's face, and she screamed, extending her fangs.

"We don't have time for this," Klaus fumed, knocking the man aside and then grabbing Rebekah by the arm to restrain her. The burns on her face were already healing. The humans might be determined, but they were only foot soldiers. There were thousands more back in New Orleans, anyway, and killing these rebels would accomplish nothing.

"We will fight to the death!" shouted a sweet-faced woman with chestnut hair, pulling a dagger from a sheath. It glinted silver in the firelight, and in spite of himself, Klaus was impressed by the preparations these humans had made.

"We'll take you up on that another time, love," Klaus promised. He elbowed the nearest man in the chest, pushing him into two of the other humans, then gestured for Rebekah to follow him.

The chestnut-haired woman ran at Rebekah with the dagger, but she only sighed, caught the woman's arm as the dagger came down, and broke it with ease. She threw the woman at the nearest humans and followed Klaus to the cabin.

The vines that covered the little house seemed to reach for them, clinging and burning wherever they touched skin. Klaus tore a handful off the wall and smelled it, ignoring the singing pain it caused to his palm. "What the hell is this stuff?"

"Let's skip the botany lesson," Rebekah suggested, pulling the vines from her golden hair and throwing them aside. "Just get Elijah and burn the place to the ground. That should sort it out."

Klaus threw his shoulder into the wooden door and it shattered inward, spraying the small room with splinters. Two tall, cloaked figures stood over a bed where Elijah lay, pale and seemingly unconscious. But his brother's face turned toward the sound of the door breaking, and his cracked lips silently formed the words *"Come in."*

The two humans turned as well. Klaus recognized his fortune-teller, and the man beside Alejandra resembled her so strongly that he could only be her brother. The man—Tomás—threw some iridescent powder at Klaus with a lightning-fast flick of his wrist, but Klaus moved even faster. He had Alejandra by the throat before Tomás's powder had even fallen to the floor. He bared his fangs dangerously close to her face.

"Your brother needs me alive," Alejandra warned, choosing her words carefully.

"Lies." Rebekah sneered, and Klaus turned to see her sitting astride Tomás, his face shoved into the powder on the floor. "There's nothing you have to offer us except your deaths, and those are close at hand."

"What my sister says is true." Tomás gasped, and Rebekah tightened her grip on the back of his neck. "Elijah is hers now—killing her will break him."

Elijah groaned, his eyes open and unseeing. Klaus eased his hold on Alejandra's throat, even though all his instincts told him not to. "Explain yourself," he ordered, backing up a step.

"Vinaya powder has allowed me to take possession

of Elijah." Alejandra smirked, although her racing heartbeat contradicted her confidence. "Soon I will have complete control of him, and he will be my instrument to break your hold on our city."

"All the more reason to kill you now," Klaus pointed out, licking the tip of a fang.

"Have you ever seen a puppet with its strings cut?" Alejandra asked, her voice cruel and a little amused. "Your brother belongs to me now, and my power sustains him. If I die, he will stay trapped in his pain. Forever."

"Nothing is forever," Rebekah said.

"I am your only chance at getting him back, and for that you need me alive," Alejandra replied with a lingering smile.

Klaus weighed her words, testing them for truth. He knew a fair amount about magic, and she'd be tremendously lucky if her powder worked as she promised. In Klaus's experience, magic was rarely so convenient. Magic had laws unto itself, and Alejandra wasn't even a witch—she was just a human who was in far over her head.

There was only one way to find out if she was telling the truth: Kill her. Klaus's eyes fixed on the pulse in Alejandra's neck, his decision made. She saw it, too, and her scream rattled the cabin's windows.

"Elijah!" she yelled. "Protect me!"

Elijah lay still on the bed. But he sprang into action at the sound of her voice, hurling himself against Klaus so hard that Klaus heard his own shoulder break against the far wall. Alejandra had told part of the truth, at least: Elijah was hers now.

"Elijah!" Rebekah cried, hurrying to her feet, Tomás momentarily forgotten. The man rolled away from her to join his sister near the hearth.

Elijah moved faster than the human eye could follow to stand between . . . the twins, Klaus realized, seeing their faces together. They had chosen the symbol of their cult to reflect their own self-image. Alejandra and Tomás weren't just humans who played at being witches—they also fancied themselves the two faces of the god Janus.

"Kill them both," the fortune-teller whispered, pulling her cloak around her slender form, and Elijah obeyed.

He was every bit as fast and as strong as if he weren't bewitched, and he managed to throw Rebekah across the room before she could make a single move to block him. She crashed into the rafters and then collapsed onto the bed, too stunned to pull herself back up.

Klaus had a little more time to brace himself for Elijah's next attack, but he didn't fare much better than their sister had. "Elijah," he began, blocking the first punch, but Elijah's second blow spun his head so hard that Klaus's spine snapped. Rebekah flew at Elijah, trying to distract him while Klaus's neck pulled itself back together, but Elijah truly was a man possessed.

For a moment, Klaus could see the White Oak stake that Rebekah had brought home with her. Nothing short of that could stop Elijah now.

"Why couldn't you just leave me alone?" Elijah demanded, catching Klaus and slamming him sideways onto the bed. It groaned and then collapsed beneath the impact. "I was happy to finally be away from you two, and you just couldn't let it be."

Then he spun to deal with Rebekah, twisting free of her grip and crushing her up against the fireplace. The hem of her gown, still wet from the swamp, began to smoke and pop. An acrid smell filled the cabin, and Klaus could see a nasty burn beginning to form on his sister's leg before she managed to fight her way free.

Tomás and Alejandra had retreated to the broken bed, watching the vampires' every move. Klaus heard their friends calling from outside, urging them to flee from the cabin, but Alejandra's face was fierce and proud. She believed that her champion could destroy their enemies, and she wanted to witness the moment Elijah overpowered his siblings.

And he would beat them—Klaus saw that clearly. Elijah *wanted* to fight, and that gave him a sizable advantage. Klaus and Rebekah only hoped to stop him, but in the grip of Alejandra's powder, Elijah wanted to destroy them.

Klaus rolled and grabbed Elijah's ankle, jerking him off his feet so that his head and hands landed in the fire. "I'm sorry," he muttered, as much to himself as to the brother who couldn't hear him.

He dug into the flesh of Elijah's back with his bare hands, trying to pull out his spine. Elijah landed a brutal kick in the center of Klaus's stomach, but Rebekah recovered enough to help. She held Elijah's face to the embers.

Klaus could tear his brother limb from limb, but it wouldn't matter. Elijah would recover from any trivial wound, and every wound was trivial to an Original. The only way to stop this—to truly end it—was to kill Alejandra and hope that she was wrong about vinaya powder.

Elijah heaved forward and shattered Rebekah's rib cage against the edge of the hearth. There was no more time to waste if Klaus and his siblings wanted to walk out of this miserable place. If he wanted to win, he would have to cut the strings that made his brother dance.

SEVENTEEN

Rebekah rubbed at her sore ribs, kicking Elijah's face almost as an afterthought. The whole fight was pointless. She didn't want to hurt Elijah, but it didn't seem like she had much of a choice. Klaus was back on his feet, and Rebekah struggled to her own, ready to coordinate their next attack, but Klaus was looking the wrong way.

Rebekah was fast, but Klaus had a head start. "Don't be an idiot!" she shouted, and then Elijah caught her ankle, holding her back. "Put an end to this," she pleaded to her older brother, wrenching her way free. "Elijah, I know you can hear me."

"I never stopped hearing you," Elijah snapped,

rolling to his feet. "I just stopped listening, little sister. What do you think drove me out of New Orleans?"

"That bitch who put a spell on you," Rebekah countered, "and Niklaus wants to kill her for it." Elijah's foot snaked around hers, tripping her as she tried to run back to Klaus.

"I'm not done with you yet, Rebekah," he snarled.

Rebekah fell to the ground, pinned under her brother's legs. She twisted, trying to free herself before Klaus did something unbelievably stupid.

"Stop!" she yelled, but Klaus didn't listen.

He closed the distance between him and Alejandra in three long strides. Alejandra began to shriek and Tomás moved in to shield her, but Klaus was an unstoppable force. Klaus ripped the woman's head from her body before Rebekah could even cry out a last warning. Blood spurted from of her neck like a hot, red fountain, covering Klaus in the grisly aftermath as her body slumped to the floor.

Elijah screamed in pain, a wordless, mindless howl that seemed to go on and on for days. Rebekah tried to embrace him, pushing back strands of brown hair and making what she hoped were soothing noises. She searched for any hint of recognition in his eyes, but he just stared at the ceiling rafters and moaned.

"Klaus," she snapped, "get over here!"

Klaus glanced at Elijah, then at Tomás, who was staring at his twin sister's head in horror. Klaus let the head drop from his hand, and it rolled to tap Tomás's foot. The man whispered something inaudible and touched the two-headed silver pin at his throat. Rebekah thought she saw wetness in his pale green eyes, although he kept rigid control of the rest of his face. The moment seemed to stretch out forever, and then Tomás broke and ran, fleeing for his life through the cabin's shattered door. Rebekah didn't want to let him go, but all she could think about was Elijah.

Klaus appeared at her side, and Rebekah fought the urge to ask him where his concern had been when he'd decided to murder their only key to unlocking their brother.

"It will pass," Klaus said, his voice taut with anxiety. "Just give him a minute while the spell wears off."

Rebekah remembered the sight of Luc, lying helplessly beneath the White Oak tree. The powder had affected him far longer than it had her, and Elijah had consumed much more of the stuff than either of them had inhaled. Klaus's recklessness might still cost them everything they were trying to save.

"It's *not* wearing off," she pointed out, resting her hand on Elijah's broad forehead. It was damp, beaded with cold sweat. He writhed in obvious agony, and his pain only added to her fury. Elijah fell silent, his jaw clenched so hard that Rebekah could see muscles standing out on the sides of his neck. "Niklaus, you have no idea what you did. What if Alejandra was telling the truth, and this is his life now?"

"Then we'll bring her back from the dead and make her reverse it," Klaus insisted, his chin jutting out stubbornly. "Or we'll find some witches and force them to help us, or we'll discover some other powder that counters this one. There's no way that letting her live was our only option, and when you're done being dramatic, you'll see that."

Rebekah wished she could bash Klaus's head in for that comment. This was all his fault, after all. He was the one who had first brought Alejandra into their lives. Even Rebekah's mistake of playing into Tomás's hands had started with Klaus. If he hadn't carelessly threatened Marguerite so many times, Rebekah might have given the murder a closer look. She sincerely hoped that he was putting all the pieces together and taking his share of the blame to heart, even if he would never admit to it aloud.

"We need to get him home at least," she muttered. "He doesn't belong out here. He should be home with us while we try to work this out."

Klaus lifted Elijah across his shoulder, taking a

moment to test his balance. Then he walked out of the cabin without another word in his own defense.

Rebekah pulled down one of the curtains and used the hearth to set it ablaze, then laid it against the flimsy wooden wall. Sparks flew and flames licked up the fabric. Soon the entire cabin was on fire. Alejandra's corpse, the dangerous vines, and any memories this place contained went up in smoke. If the humans needed a reminder of what happened when you crossed the Originals, then this pile of ashes would have to serve.

The fire caught quickly, spreading along the thin walls and growing brighter as it overtook the rafters. Rebekah smelled something bitter when the first of the vines began to burn, and she hurried from the cabin with the sleeve of her gown pressed over her mouth and nose.

The humans were long gone. Rebekah had no doubt that Tomás was rounding them up right now, and he would recruit new rebels the moment he returned to New Orleans. He would want to avenge his sibling. Anyone would.

Rebekah and Klaus rowed their way back along the stagnant river, refusing to inhale deeply until they had climbed up out of the bayou at last. Rebekah remained alert for any sign that they were being watched. The humans had gotten the upper hand too many times thanks to the Mikaelsons' inattention, and she was done being complacent.

Lisette was seated on the front steps of the mansion when they arrived, looking like a child who'd been locked out of the house. Rebekah frankly couldn't understand what had gone wrong between her and Elijah. Lisette had always been a good friend to her, and Rebekah couldn't imagine her doing anything to deserve the pain her break with Elijah had put her through.

"Open the door, Lisette," Rebekah called out, unable to stand the sight of the vampire looking so lost and hopeless.

"Hurry," Klaus added as Lisette jumped to her feet. "Elijah needs rest."

"We have no idea *what* he needs," Rebekah said, unwilling to let Klaus forget his crime so easily, "and the only person who does know is dead."

"I'm sure we can torture it out of Tomás if we need to," Klaus answered, angling his body to bring Elijah through the front door without knocking him against the frame. "But I doubt that will even be necessary. He'll recover now that the bitch's fingers are out of his brain."

Elijah shuddered and groaned, and Lisette's pale hand caught at Rebekah's sleeve. "What does he mean?" she asked, her voice trembling a little as her gaze tracked every second of Klaus's progress up the curving staircase. "Was it his . . . his new . . . I mean, what was done to him?"

"He's been possessed," Rebekah explained, shaking out her burnt and muddy petticoats with a heavy sigh. "And yes, Alejandra Vargas is the one who's responsible, and she has already answered for her crime. Unfortunately, before she died, she told us that the possession wouldn't end with her death. Klaus thought that was a lie, but I think we can all see that it was not."

"Possessed," Lisette whispered. Rebekah rested her hand on the vampire's shoulder. Lisette's gray eyes never left Klaus's back, even as she gave Rebekah a sad smile. "She was a witch, then?"

"She seems to know some." Rebekah frowned. The twins were alarmingly well informed and well supplied for humans, and she suspected that was another unfortunate result of the Originals growing too comfortable in New Orleans. Humans shouldn't even know about vampires' existence, much less how to fight them. Rebekah knew that was partially her fault. The Mikaelsons had grown careless, and that would have to change if they wanted to survive. "She had no magic of her own, but she and her brother had a generous supply of something called vinaya powder."

"What a strange name." Lisette frowned. "What do we know about it?"

"Not much," Rebekah admitted. Even after seeing it at work and experiencing its effects for herself, the substance was still a mystery. All she really knew was that she wanted to destroy it, along with every human whose hands had ever touched the vile powder.

Lisette bit her lip and pulled away. "I'll go pull books in Elijah's study," she called over her shoulder. "I'm of more use there than at his bedside."

Rebekah didn't argue. It couldn't hurt to learn more about their enemies' powder, and Lisette's worried look only made Rebekah more troubled.

A pained cry came from Elijah's bedroom, and Rebekah hurried upstairs. Klaus's full mouth was drawn in concern as Rebekah reached Elijah's bedside. She took one of her brother's hands in each of hers. Elijah's was unnaturally cold, and damp with sweat.

"Come back to us, brother," Rebekah whispered, feeling the full weight of her fears descend on her heart. What if the real Elijah never did return? How would she survive without him?

EIGHTEEN

Elijah felt like his entire body was on fire. It was impossible to distinguish his hallucinations from real life. His entire world had become dreams and shadows, and he wandered through them in endless pain. Alejandra was gone. Her absence left a gaping hole in Elijah—there was nothing left of him but a burning that filled every part his mind. It was impossible to move without her, impossible to live. Yet here he was, somehow alive, despite everything.

He could hear his siblings calling to him, but he had no idea how to find them. He was trapped in an infinite forest that sometimes became a swamp, although the merciless sun beat down on the back of his neck, making the place feel like an endless desert.

Sometimes his mother was there, and once he was sure that he saw his father gripping a White Oak stake from behind a hawthorn tree. As Elijah ran, Mikael stalked him through tall swamp grasses, his face hidden by shadows.

"I'm here," Rebekah whispered in Elijah's ear, and he could feel that Klaus was nearby, too. He had seen Klaus . . . he had *fought* him. First at the Southern Spot, then again, with Alejandra riding him like a broken horse. She had been inside his head, filling every corner of his mind with her voice, her scent, and her relentless will. She had told him his siblings were done with him, that they were better off without him.

But she was wrong. Rebekah and Klaus were with him now, and that had to mean something. Elijah struggled to open his eyes, to see if his siblings were really by his side, but it felt like red-hot pins had been pushed through his eyelids, fixing them in place.

Every muscle in his body strained against his closed eyelids, and he felt them lightly twitch. Somewhere above him either his mother or Rebekah gasped in surprise. It was working. He worked harder, fighting against the blank space that used to be Alejandra, and his eyes fluttered open at last.

The ceiling above him looked like the one in his own bedroom, which meant he was hallucinating. Elijah knew he was still in the cabin, and that he would probably never be allowed to leave. Alejandra had told him so, yesterday or the day before or the day before that.

Two pairs of concerned blue eyes stared down at him. He'd brought his two siblings together at last, another sign that this wasn't really happening.

"You're safe," Klaus assured him. His forehead was creased with worry. "You're home, and you're going to be all right." He felt Klaus's hand on his shoulder, and the weight and feel of his skin felt real. Was he actually in his room? Was he safe?

"Can you speak?" Rebekah asked. "Alejandra said she used vinaya powder on you, but I'd never even heard of the stuff until a few days ago. We need to know what she did in order to reverse it."

Elijah tested his lips and tongue, trying to guess how his voice might sound if he managed to force it out of his dry, cracked throat. "Thirsty," he rasped, and Rebekah jumped up at once.

"I'll go get someone for you," she said, and then she disappeared from view.

He was almost sure now that he really was awake. He could feel the softness of the mattress beneath him, and the smell of fresh flowers in the room. Nothing in his dreams had been so difficult as opening his eyes had been, and none of his hallucinations had stayed put for as long as this.

Even Rebekah had left in the usual way, by announcing her departure and then walking away, instead of hovering or vanishing or turning into someone else. He really was in his own bed . . . but that meant the pain that seared every inch of his body was real as well.

"Your Alejandra played a lot of games, brother," Klaus remarked, and Elijah could hear the resentment seething beneath his casual tone. "She divided us, and intended to have us at each other's throats in the hope that she wouldn't have to kill us all herself."

She didn't have far to go when it came to me and you, Elijah thought. *She got too close.*

"I think she had something to do with that nasty little scene between us before you left," Klaus went on. "You thought I was working with the werewolves against *you*, didn't you? We were trying to take out Janus, but my guess is that she filled you with a bunch of half-truths and sent you to the Southern Spot at just the right time to hear just the wrong things."

Elijah struggled to remember what had happened with Klaus at the brothel. What, exactly, had he overheard? What had he and Klaus said to each other during their confrontation? The memory was hazy and indistinct, like everything else in Elijah's brain at the moment.

Then he felt the sheer scope of Alejandra's betrayal at last, undermining everything he had come to believe over the past few weeks. She had lied about *everything*, but her cunning went further than that. Elijah had believed her when she said Rebekah had run off and Klaus was plotting against him, but they had never forsaken him. It was he who had failed them.

"I'm sorry," Elijah said after a long moment, and Klaus nodded, his mouth in a firm line.

Rebekah returned, holding the wrist of a young blonde woman with large, doe-like eyes. She looked vaguely familiar, and Elijah had a dim memory of blood that tasted like strawberries and sandalwood. She gasped a little when Rebekah opened the inside of her arm, which suggested that she wasn't under the control of a vampire's compulsion. She was simply a willing volunteer, another human who had been pulled into their world.

Elijah drank gratefully from the girl's wrist. He could feel her blood coursing through his own veins, soothing and repairing some of the horrible damage Alejandra and her powder had wrought.

Some, but not all. No matter how much he drank,

Elijah couldn't seem to chase away the misery that Alejandra's absence had left behind. Even worse, he couldn't drink away the sting of her betrayal, or the knowledge that he had given his heart to someone who had proven so thoroughly undeserving of it. He grew stronger on the girl's blood, but although he drank until she swayed on her feet and her lips were tinged with blue, Elijah couldn't consume enough to feel whole.

"That's enough for now," Rebekah decided, watching the girl's face critically. "Sloane, go downstairs and get some rest."

"Good. Now that that's out of the way, we have much to discuss," Klaus began after the girl fled unsteadily from the room. "Tomás is still out there somewhere, and he's infiltrated our lives to an alarming degree. I think we should—"

"Shut up, Niklaus," Rebekah snapped. With the human out of sight and mind, her deep blue eyes were riveted on Elijah's. "Don't you see? He's still in pain. Even half the blood in that poor girl's body wasn't enough to undo what you did to him."

"Alejandra?" Elijah said as firmly as he could. The sound of her name made his heart clench, but he needed to keep his siblings focused. The humans had already gained an alarming head start, and the last thing the Originals needed was to keep fighting with one another. They might as well un-dagger Kol and Finn while they were at it, and send a ship to fetch Mikael.

"Your beloved brother tore her head from her shoulders," Rebekah said coldly, and Elijah felt that space again, that emptiness in his mind where his former lover had once been. It hurt more than anything he had ever experienced. And somewhere beneath it, in a place that was difficult to drag up through the pain, was a sensation almost like grief. He missed her. He wanted her back.

"Alejandra warned us that killing her wouldn't save you, that it would only make things worse. She said her death would break something inside of you," Rebekah finished.

Klaus looked as close to unsure as Elijah had ever seen him. "That two-faced palm reader did nothing but lie," he argued. "Elijah just needs a few more moments to let the blood work, that's all. Brother, try to sit up."

His mind had cleared a bit, and his limbs felt stronger. With tremendous effort, Elijah made it to his elbows, then pushed up to a seated position. But as soon as he was upright, his head began to spin. Rebekah caught his shoulders before he collapsed.

"Close enough," she said, sharing a look with Klaus.

"Vinaya powder," Elijah said, testing the lips and

tongue. They were beginning to feel like they belonged to him again. "It was made to be a weapon. Against us."

The other two fell silent for a moment, considering the implications of what he'd said. They'd all grown accustomed to being nearly invincible. Even injuries that could kill common vampires didn't affect the Mikaelsons.

The very idea that something could have been *created* to destroy them felt wrong, dissonant with everything they had come to believe about the world. A White Oak stake could kill them and Klaus's silver daggers could put them in a deep sleep, but there had never been another weapon that could truly harm them. Until now.

Elijah licked his dry lips, summoning the strength to continue. "Vinaya was supposed to be a legend. Centuries ago, witches worked a spell on a vine that grows on the other side of the world, imbuing it with power. Supposedly it grew beyond their intentions or control, but no one has ever proven it even exists."

"There was a strange plant that grew over that cabin in the bayou. But that cabin is gone now, and the vine with it," Rebekah assured him. "Tomás won't be able to make more vinaya, and he can't have taken that much with him when he fled."

"Good," Elijah said, and took a deep breath. He

tried to suppress the part of himself that wished there was more powder, and Alejandra to feed it to him. He knew that was only the spell that had woven itself into his mind, but its grip was strong.

"But if the vine was enchanted, witches must have been the ones to do it," Rebekah guessed, brushing some honey-colored strands of hair away from her face. "We still have a few of those left around here. Perhaps they know something about this kind of magic."

"The last people I want to involve in this mess are the witches," Klaus muttered, jumping up from his chair to pace across the Turkish carpet. "There are no more witches left in this city as far as I'm concerned."

"This isn't the time to be stubborn," Rebekah replied. "They're still out there in that sad little town they built on the swamp, and they might be able to help Elijah."

"They might," Elijah agreed. The more he spoke, the stronger his voice felt. "Vinaya is their legend as much as ours. Maybe more."

"Finding an antidote isn't worth the cost of dealing with the witches," Klaus said. "I won't do it."

Elijah gripped the quilt with both fists, trying to control the surge of his emotions. He needed Klaus on his side now, so naturally Klaus would choose this moment to turn his back on his brother. "You say you were never my enemy, Niklaus, but if that's true, then act like it," he urged. "I can't stay trapped like this forever."

Klaus refused to look at him.

"Even if it means negotiating with the witches; even if it means throwing yourself at their feet and begging them for a cure," Elijah pressed. "You have to do this for me."

Klaus looked furious and clenched his jaw—as if that was the only thing that prevented him from refusing outright. But to put his pride before his vow to his family would be unforgivable. All three of them knew that.

"I'll go today," Klaus agreed at last, and Elijah sank back against his pillows, his breath short and his heart heavy.

NINETEEN

"It should be right here," Klaus grumbled, feeling at the empty air in front of him and cursing his siblings' stubbornness yet again. He had never had a reason to seek out the witches' hidden compound until now, and he would have been just as happy never to know where it was.

Sampson Collado scanned the ground. "I don't see anything there," he said, and Klaus fought the urge to simply snap his neck.

"It's *invisible*," he reminded the werewolf, drawing out the word in case Sampson needed to hear it more slowly. "Not seeing it is the entire point."

"There must be *something* to see." Sampson shrugged.

He had spent the last half hour insisting that the witches must have some kind of marker at the entrance. As if they *wanted* visitors, as if he and Klaus would be welcomed with open arms. "Does that yellowish stone look out of place to you?"

"It does not." The field was full of stones, and they all looked exactly the same. Klaus was already out of sorts and Sampson wasn't helping. He hated that he was being pressured to deal with the witches who had delighted in his torment twenty-two years before. It was even more irritating to have to bring a werewolf puppy along as well. But a show of unity might help inspire the witches to cooperate, and Sampson had argued that point persuasively. How would it look if their ancestral enemy—the vampires—had shown up alone, demanding to strike yet another doomed bargain? Klaus had to agree that even the witches weren't that stupid.

Rebekah could have come along, if only to show Klaus where the witches' concealment spell began, but she had made a great, melodramatic show of refusing to leave Elijah's bedside. It was as if she cared more about making her point than about Elijah's actual well-being, a revelation that Klaus hoped would not be lost on their brother. Klaus might have made some mistakes, but at least now he was acting to correct them, rather than lazing about in the mansion, trying to teach some kind of abstract lesson.

Klaus's hand struck something solid, although all he could see was open air. The bayou appeared totally undisturbed, full of buzzing insects, waving grasses, and squelching black mud. But there was something else there, right in front of them, and Klaus slid his hand sideways along the invisible wall until he found an opening. "Here," he announced, and without another glance at Sampson, he stepped through into the witches' compound.

He blinked at the sight of the town that appeared, and couldn't resist checking over his shoulder to make sure that the clearing in the bayou was still out there, just as it had been a moment before. Sampson came through the gateway beside him, looking a bit sullen at not having found the way himself, and the two of them made their way to the center of the compound in a silence that was not especially companionable.

They had made no secret of their arrival, and the witches were waiting for them when they reached the long, low meetinghouse that stood at the center of the village. Lily Leroux's power play had done nothing to improve the living conditions of her people, which Klaus found gratifying in a way. He still would have preferred to see them entirely wiped off the map, never to plague him again.

Lily's former chair was occupied by a new witch, who Klaus hoped was more rational than her predecessor. Her raven hair was shot through with silver, and Klaus could see the remnants of what must have been great beauty in the elegant lines of her face. "Greetings," she said, with no trace of warmth or encouragement. "My name is Amalia Giroux, and of course we all recognize your face here, vampire."

She turned pointedly to Sampson, who cleared his throat uncomfortably under the witch's stern gaze. "My name is Sampson Collado, and I represent the werewolves of New Orleans," he said.

Klaus shifted, preparing to speak, but Sampson couldn't seem to stop talking. "We have come to you—together—because of a threat that affects all of us," the young werewolf went on, and Klaus clenched his teeth together.

Grandstanding aside, the matter was simple. Witches—if not the same ones assembled here, then their brothers and sisters elsewhere—had sold supernatural weapons to a malicious bunch of humans. The problem properly belonged to Amalia, and Klaus had come to lay it at her feet. But there was no denying that Sampson's phrasing was more diplomatic, and with Elijah's health on the line, Klaus knew this wasn't the moment to settle old scores.

"We have heard this sort of claim before," Amalia countered, feigning disinterest in Sampson's words. "No good has ever come to our clan from trusting either of your kinds. We once stood on equal footing with the Navarro werewolves, ruling New Orleans together, and you can see what has become of us since then."

"The Navarros are long dead," Klaus reminded her. The witches had raised a deadly hurricane to cleanse the city of their enemies, although in the end it had been Klaus who had destroyed the werewolves when they laid siege to his house. "But it is the humans of this city who strive to replace them now, and they have amassed powerful weapons against all of us. Right now my brother suffers under the influence of something called vinaya powder, and that is only one of the many tools these rebels possess. They intend to drive everything supernatural out of New Orleans and reclaim it for themselves. They won't stop with the vampires and werewolves—you'll be next."

"There's no love lost between us," Sampson pointed out. "*Any* of us," he emphasized, with a sideways nod toward Klaus. "But we have shared this city for generations, and however we might fight among ourselves, I think we can all agree that none of us want the humans to take it from us."

Klaus had to admit that his own arguments sounded that much more convincing when they came from his enemy's mouth. Even Amalia seemed like she could be persuaded, but he knew her price would be high.

"Vinaya powder," Amalia repeated, brushing aside Sampson's speech as if it were irrelevant. Her cool facade slipped enough to show Klaus her surprise at his allegation. "That's a myth, at least as far as those of us here know. These humans of yours must be well connected to have found such a thing."

"That makes them dangerous to all of us," Klaus pointed out. "My brother Elijah needs your help to figure out a cure. Healing him would be a gesture of goodwill that could allow us to unite and to put an end to this threat."

Amalia laughed, a sound that rippled like molten silver. "I know of a way to free a vampire from the powder you speak of," she admitted, "but I will need a bit more than an alliance with you in exchange."

Klaus had expected as much, but showed his displeasure with a raised eyebrow and a smirk. He had a reputation to maintain, after all. "What sort of extortion did you have in mind, then?" he asked, his voice deceptively mild. "What is more important to you than the goodwill of my family, after all that your kind has done to mine?"

"You and I have no personal history," Amalia reminded him, her spine straight. "Every witch who ever dealt with you here is dead now, and all their kin with them. If you wish to bargain with *me*, Klaus Mikaelson, then you need to bring something more than hurt feelings to the table. I suggest a place in our ancestral city, equal to yours and the werewolves'."

"That's not his to offer," Sampson argued hotly, stepping forward. "New Orleans doesn't belong to the vampires, and it isn't his to give away. If you want a place there, witch, then act on its behalf, the way any deserving leader would."

Amalia didn't even look at the pup. Instead her gaze remained, steady and unblinking, on Klaus. She knew perfectly well that he had the power to deliver what she asked for, and that it was a fair price in exchange for the life of his brother.

"Consider it done," he said, ignoring the seething glare Sampson shot his way. Building a lasting peace wasn't Klaus's job, and it wasn't his concern. He simply had to get through one crisis at a time. When Elijah was better, they could face the next challenge together, as family. "Cure Elijah, and you can return to New Orleans."

"As equals," Amalia prompted. "No good has ever come from one of our kinds growing too powerful.

I truly am not seeking to take advantage of your misfortune, vampire, or else I would ask for more. But neither will I accept less than what you already have, nor less than what your brother offered the werewolves decades ago."

"Equals it is," Klaus repeated, feeling his jaw clench around the words. "Just tell me how to free my brother from the control of that cursed powder."

Amalia gestured to one of the witches who stood at the edge of the meeting hall. She ducked out through the low wooden doorframe and hurried away along the gravel path. "Ruth will bring you everything we have written on the subject of vinaya," Amalia explained, "so that you can understand what I am about to tell you. Because as little as you liked my terms, Klaus, I think you'll like what I know about vinaya powder even less."

"Don't tell me the effects can't be reversed," Klaus warned, taking an instinctive inventory of the room in case this parlay came to violence after all. "I beheaded the last woman who told me that."

"I assume that was the woman who was using the vinaya magic to possess your brother," Amalia pointed out, raising one black eyebrow sardonically. "That was ill done, as I'm sure you've realized by now. It's left your brother in agonizing pain, and if he were anything less than an Original, that pain would have killed him by now. It would have killed a hundred lesser vampires, and yet your brother endures his suffering."

"Not for long," Klaus reminded her. "You're going to tell me how to cure him."

"Yes," Amalia agreed, pressing the tips of her long fingers together. "That I will." She gestured to the doorway, where Ruth had reappeared with a small stack of dense-looking books. They were exactly the sort of thing Elijah might have pored over to find some convoluted solution. But Klaus's tastes ran more toward immediate action, and as Ruth approached he eyed the books with distaste.

"If you know how it's done, then simply do it," he suggested, increasingly wary of Amalia's caginess. She was supposed to be giving him *good* news, and yet she didn't act that way at all. "You say you want a seat at the table, and yet when I ask for a spell, you hide behind riddles and books?"

"I want to make sure you understand the sacrifice that Elijah's cure will require," Amalia replied. She took the stack of books from Ruth and pulled a thin, silvery candle from the folds of her cloak. Her face was so grave that Klaus nearly burst out laughing. It was ridiculous to think that he would care about some sacrifice now, after everything that had already been taken from him over the last thousand years. It didn't matter what dire warnings Amalia had to give him along with Elijah's cure; all Klaus cared about was that there *was* a cure. "Listen closely, Niklaus," Amalia went on, still refusing to so much as smile, "and I will explain what that human woman's death is going to cost you."

TWENTY

Rebekah was in Mystic Falls again. She ran alongside a herd of deer, straining to make her own feet fly as fast as their pounding hooves. At any moment she would rise free of the earth itself, and join the hawks that circled the soft white clouds. Her family watched her from the cabin, Esther smiling in the sunlight.

She had everything she could possibly need, except her heart knew that none of it was real. Luc was somewhere ahead of her, calling to her, waiting to intercept her and drag her back into what had become of her life. He waved his arms, warning her to slow down, but Rebekah believed that if she kept running, she might still take flight and escape him.

"Rebekah," he repeated, and she realized he was beside her, holding her arm, pinning her like a butterfly under glass.

"I'm here," she answered, startling awake. Luc stood over her, his hand resting on her shoulder and his blue eyes concerned. Rebekah blinked at the sight of Elijah's bedroom, all gray and gold, with the French doors opened onto the balcony to let in the cool night air.

Elijah lay on his bed, his eyes closed against whatever terrible pain caused him to twitch and thrash. Rebekah regretted dozing off, but she could tell at a glance that little had changed for him.

"How long have you been by his side?" Luc asked, frowning with concern. "When was the last time you ate? You're never so slow to wake. I worry that you aren't caring for yourself as you should."

"I can't leave. I promised Klaus that I would stay with Elijah," Rebekah said, taking in Luc's muddy clothes and tousled hair. "Where have you been all this time?" she asked.

It had been days since she had last seen him, she realized. She wasn't even sure where he had been during their search for Elijah, and the handsome pirate had been conspicuously absent from her side ever since. Rebekah had been too focused on Elijah to notice much or care, but it was poor form nonetheless.

Luc stared at her in surprise, then glanced at Elijah's unconscious form. "I was pursuing Tomás, of course," he said.

It actually did look as though he had been tracking some renegade human through the bayou for days. Rebekah was grateful for his help, but part of her wished he had been here, keeping watch with her. His fingers still lingered on her arm, and she wanted to ease into his touch.

"No one asked you to do that," she said. "How did you even know Tomás was in New Orleans? The last you saw of him was in Virginia, days away from here."

"He said he would destroy everything that you loved until he was ready to kill you," Luc said, the threat making even his warm, joyful voice sound ominous. "I never thought he intended to do those things from a distance . . . did you?"

"Of course not," Rebekah admitted, although something still nagged at her. With all of the plots and schemes that had ensnared her family recently, it was growing difficult to trust anyone. Even the most open, uncomplicated vampire she had ever met suddenly looked sinister, looming over her and Elijah. "Why didn't you tell me, though? A lot has happened here, and I would have liked you with me."

"I see that," Luc agreed, running his fingers along her arm and up to her shoulder. "I didn't mean for my absence to hurt you, Rebekah. I promise you I would rather have spent every moment with you. But two nights ago, I met a group of werewolves in a tavern. They told me all about the search for Elijah, and that you and your brother were tracking a lead into the bayou. I had a feeling that Tomás might be involved with Elijah's disappearance, and if I was right, I wanted to see where he would run next."

"That was an ambitious play," Rebekah observed, surprised. Luc had always seemed like a man who preferred to swim along with the current, rather than someone who laid his own plans. She wondered if she had misjudged him, or whether his encounter with Tomás had changed him. "Did you meet with any success?"

"Only some hints and rumors," Luc answered, his eyes flicking to Elijah and then the open French doors before returning to Rebekah's own. "I wish I had better news. But I'd rather return to you with nothing than keep chasing shadows through the city for another night. I've missed you, my Rebekah." His fingers drew circles along her back, his touch electric through the fabric of her silk gown.

"I'm glad you came back." Rebekah smiled, feeling the weariness of watching over Elijah begin to fall away. The world became an entirely different place when there was someone in it just for her, to support her as she had so often supported her brothers. This was what it might feel like to have a family of her own someday, to be surrounded by people who were attuned to her needs rather than warring brothers who constantly created new problems out of thin air.

Luc stroked a loose lock of her hair away from her face, tucking it gently behind her ear. For a moment she remembered the feel of Tomás's mouth against her own, so vividly that he might have been standing before her again. She shivered a little, and reached up to hold Luc's hand against her cheek. "How could I have stayed away?" he asked, more softly, his eyes locked on hers.

Rebekah let him draw her to her feet, and she made her way into the hallway almost by feel—she was too wrapped up in kissing Luc to properly look where she was going. "Go fetch Lisette," she called to a human butler who waited silently at the top of the spiral staircase. "Tell her that it's her turn to sit with Elijah."

The man sprang into action, spurred on by the power of Rebekah's compulsion.

Luc swept her up into his arms, carrying her the rest of the way to her room, so that all she had to think about was the sweet, salty taste of his lips.

The door of Rebekah's room burst inward under the weight of Luc's shoulder, and when they were through, Rebekah's foot shot out to kick it shut. Moonlight streamed in through the windows, and her bed had never looked so inviting. Luc swung her onto the soft silk sheets, and then he kissed her more deeply than before—as if even the brief second when their mouths were apart had been too much for him to bear.

"Undress me," she whispered, pulling him onto her as she lay back on the pillows.

Luc obliged, forgoing the dozens of buttons that ran down the seams of her bodice in favor of simply tearing it open. She heard the boning on her corset snap under the insistent pressure of his hands, and then her skin was bare to the cool air.

Luc's hot mouth chased the chill away, as with his hands he pulled Rebekah free of the last shreds of her gown and underthings. She tore at his clothes as well, pinned by the weight of his body pressing down on her, but desperate to feel the heat of his tan skin against hers.

Luc kissed her so passionately that Rebekah thought she might drown in him. She couldn't see, hear, or breathe anything except for him. For the briefest of moments she realized that she had very nearly died almost exactly this way, that Luc had filled every inch of her vision just before he had driven the White Oak stake into her heart.

In the instant when he entered her, she felt the same shock as she had in that moment; trapped between Luc's brawny form and the White Oak tree. Rebekah saw stars wheeling overhead through the ceiling of her room, and the steady motion of Luc's hips made it seem as though her bed were adrift on the ocean.

She pulled him closer, tasting salt on his skin and wrapping her legs around his trim waist, trying to hold on to him through the visions that played in her head. This was why she had wanted to live. This feeling, this connection, this moment were what had made her life too good to give up.

She had remained alive in order to love, and every inch of her body loved Luc's. His breath came fast and ragged, and she could feel her own heartbeat speeding up to match his, binding them together even more closely.

But Rebekah still couldn't quite shut out the feeling of being somewhere else. Her pleasure was just too much to be contained by any four walls, and when she climaxed she could feel the entire world pulse and hum along with her body.

Luc finished just a moment after she did, and he collapsed beside her on the bed. "I should never have left your side," he said, reaching across to caress the delicate skin of her stomach.

Rebekah smiled up at the ceiling, confident that he wouldn't make the same mistake again.

TWENTY-ONE

At the sound of the door slamming shut, Elijah's eyes flew open. He had very little strength left, but he had been hoarding it, conserving what he had for the moment when he was finally alone. Rebekah had been hopelessly attentive, staying at his bedside as if she were some strange plant that had grown there, but as soon as he heard her new plaything enter the room, Elijah had steadied himself for the task ahead.

It was almost impossible to pull himself up to sitting, but when he swung his legs over the edge of his bed, standing up wasn't quite as difficult as he had expected. He placed one foot in front of the other, reminding his legs how to work. By the time he reached his door, he felt almost like his old self again, except for the terrible, overwhelming, unavoidable compulsion that was driving him out of the mansion.

Elijah silently opened the door and slipped out into the hallway, every sense alert. He could hear Rebekah a few doors away, thoroughly engaged. Elijah blocked out the sound, because somewhere in the distance Alejandra was calling to him, assuring him that Klaus and Rebekah had lied about her fate. She wasn't dead, left to rot in the middle of the bayou; she was just outside of the house, waiting for him in the gardens.

Or perhaps she was just a bit farther than that. She couldn't have stepped past the barrier of the protection spell that still surrounded the house without attracting notice. Elijah only needed to get outside its circle and then he would be able to see his love again.

He *needed* to see her; he could barely breathe without her. He went down the hall, toward the great curving front staircase, feeling stronger by the second. His footsteps were silent and sure as he descended the marble steps. He couldn't have resisted Alejandra's call even if he had wanted to, but surely it had to mean something that his vitality had returned when he was on his way to meet her.

A door creaked on its hinges somewhere in the

south wing, and Elijah froze, trying to make the outline of his body melt into the shadows at the base of the staircase. He listened, but whoever was moving around the ground floor was as stealthy as he was. Even this brief pause made him feel dizzy, and he could feel his heart pounding in his chest. He *needed* to get beyond the protection spell.

If they found him, they would try to stop him. How could he have ever thought his siblings were on his side? Rebekah and Klaus were traitors who held him back, used him, and made him a prisoner in his own home. They didn't want him to be happy, didn't want him to be with Alejandra. No one understood what Elijah had to do, and their misguided good intentions would only bring more violence and pain.

Long after he had lost count of his heartbeats, Elijah finally risked a step forward. He could almost smell the painted wood of the front door, not to mention the glorious freedom that lay beyond it.

The grand front hall was empty and silent. Moonlight slanted in at a curious angle that made half the marble glow brilliantly white, while the rest was so black there might have been nothing in its place but emptiness. The moon was nearly full, Elijah realized in surprise, wondering at the way the weeks had slipped away from him.

He would be back in control of his mind and his life

soon enough. All he needed to do was rejoin Alejandra, and the door was directly before him. He reached for it, so eager to be out in the open air—

"Where do you think you're going?" Lisette demanded, and before Elijah could even turn toward her she had thrown herself between him and the handle of the front door. His skin began to prickle and then burn. He had to obey. He had to leave.

"Get out of my way," he warned, hoping that she would listen. Once upon a time, he would have been able to force her, to use his own magic to control her mind and move her aside. But there was no chance of that now, not in his weakened state. If he couldn't convince Lisette to let him go, then Elijah would need to fight his way past her, and there was no part of him that looked forward to that.

"I went upstairs to sit with you and you were gone," she said, showing no sign of planning to step aside. "Elijah, you need to rest."

"I need some air," he disagreed, his limbs itching as if every inch of them were being viciously stung by insects. Elijah rubbed at his arms, wishing that Lisette would just go away and stop tormenting him. She had been haunting him for months, and it was no surprise that she had chosen to confront him now. He was finally happy with another woman, and Lisette couldn't bear that. She was interfering intentionally to keep him from Alejandra, with no regard for the physical agony it was causing him to be apart from her.

Even worse, Lisette was peering even more closely at him, inspecting each of his eyes for signs of distress. "Something is wrong with you," she murmured, lifting her hand to tilt his chin for a better look.

Elijah felt a sudden blaze of rage explode within his chest, and he threw Lisette so hard that her back splintered the door. She landed heavily, and Elijah leaped over her, his eyes on the trees at the far edge of the manicured lawns. The protection spell stopped there, and he could almost taste the freedom that lay on its other side.

A hand wrapped around his ankle as he jumped over the veranda steps, and dirt and gravel filled his mouth as he crashed to the ground. Lisette scrabbled for a better hold, clutching at his burning arms and the back of his head in a desperate bid to bring him back under her control.

Elijah rolled and caught her by the neck, intending to choke her until she was unconscious, but the pain that wracked his body was only getting worse. The burst of strength that had carried him out of the mansion disappeared, and Lisette broke free, pinning him to the ground with a viselike grip.

"Stay down," she ordered, her voice hoarse from the damage he had managed to inflict on her throat. He stared at the handprint he had left imprinted on her skin. "Elijah, I think that the powder is still working in you."

That conclusion was so obvious that Elijah could have murdered her on the spot for being so slow. The cursed powder filled every part of him, torturing him with no hope of respite. The only way to end its hold on him would be to reach Alejandra, and Lisette refused to let him go. He struggled wildly, trying to shake her off, but the pain had crept back into his brain, and his limbs refused to do what he wanted.

"It must be Tomás," Lisette said, holding Elijah's hands over his head and looking into the forest. She scanned the trees for a sign of the human, but was searching for the wrong twin. "Elijah, this is important. You have to fight this and stay here with me."

Everything in Elijah told him to do the exact opposite: that getting free of Lisette and away the mansion was the most important thing he could do. But her voice stirred something buried and half forgotten—the long-lost memories of a woman he had once loved. He'd shoved those memories deep down into the well of his heart and tried to banish them from his mind, but his feelings for Lisette had never fully disappeared.

And so when the vinaya provoked him again, commanding him to kill Lisette and move on, Elijah found himself resisting its pull. In spite of the desire that literally burned him from the inside out, he knew that Lisette must not become a casualty of Alejandra's magic. It was bad enough that Elijah had turned his back on her, that he had tried to forget her in the arms of a human who had turned out to be his enemy. He had already hurt Lisette far too badly, and no matter what Alejandra's ghost whispered in his ear, he absolutely refused to do any worse. Lisette deserved better from him, and that truth drove Elijah to resist the vinaya's control.

As he lay on his back, with Lisette above him, he relaxed. He felt the dampness of the crushed grass beneath him seep into his clothes. He reminded himself of what he knew to be real: Alejandra was dead, and before she died she had taken control of him. She lured him with empty promises, and now, looking up at the real, true promise of Lisette, he knew it.

He closed his eyes and let Alejandra drift away from him again. Sensing the change in him, Lisette loosened her grip. "I should have said something sooner," she said. "I could tell that you were different, and when Klaus told me about that woman, I knew she must be bad for you. But I was still angry, and perhaps a bit jealous, and I didn't press the matter the way I should have. I was afraid you would dismiss my fears as nothing but the resentment of a former lover."

"I would have," Elijah admitted, finding his voice again at last. "But I'm glad you didn't simply leave me to my fate. I didn't deserve this kindness after the way I treated you."

"You did what you thought you had to do," Lisette said. "I don't know that it was the *right* thing, but that doesn't really matter anymore. When you need me, I will be here, and nothing is going to change that."

Hearing her words made some of his pain disappear. It wouldn't dissipate completely—this agony was brutal and unrelenting and seemed determined to be his own personal hell for the rest of eternity—but Lisette's wry smile made it recede ever so slightly. Lisette was strong, and she had just proved herself strong enough for both of them. He had always regretted hurting her, but for the first time he sincerely regretted leaving her. He wondered if there might have been another way, if he could have protected her from Klaus without forsaking her entirely.

"What is this?" Klaus demanded, as if by thinking about his brother, Elijah had caused him to appear. "Lisette, what the hell were you thinking bringing him out here?"

"I'm the one who stopped him," she countered, and Elijah thought she seemed a little reluctant to separate from him as she rose to her feet to face Klaus. "I was watching your back once again, you spoiled ingrate."

To Elijah's surprise, Klaus didn't lash out in return; perhaps the two of them had come to some kind of understanding. An uneasy one, from the look of things, but even a shaky rapport was better than murderous hatred. "I've never known you to watch anything of mine when Elijah was in the room, love," Klaus replied sardonically, and Elijah noticed that Klaus held a small stack of dusty books loosely under one arm. "Bring him back inside, will you? While you were frolicking about on the lawns, I seem to have found a cure for my brother's affliction."

Elijah closed his eyes in relief as the two of them lifted him, each wrapping one of his arms around their shoulders. He had made it; he had outlasted Alejandra's curse. Klaus's visit to the witches had been a success, and soon Elijah would be his own man once again.

TWENTY-TWO

*T*he sun was rising over the eastern hills, and human servants hurried around the mansion closing shutters and drawing curtains against its painful rays. Klaus watched a particularly fetching young maid as she barred the last set of wooden shutters in the salon, studying her lithe movements as he tried to shut out all his other thoughts. The maid glanced coyly over her shoulder before leaving the room, but no flirtation could lighten Klaus's mood that morning.

Rebekah appeared in the doorway just after the maid passed through, her hair a bit tangled and her cheeks unnaturally flushed. Klaus raised an eyebrow at the sight of her, easily guessing how she had passed the night. "I hope you've been enjoying yourself, dear sister," he greeted her, his voice dangerously light. "While you were otherwise engaged, I found Elijah wandering the gardens."

Rebekah's mouth dropped open in shock, leaving her uncharacteristically speechless. It wouldn't last long, Klaus knew, but he relished her guilty silence as long as he could.

"I'm all right," Elijah murmured, his trembling voice betraying the lie. He lay awkwardly across a scrolled wooden bench, his head resting in Lisette's lap. In her usual way, Lisette seemed to have no awareness whatsoever that she didn't belong in this council, or that her presence among the three siblings might be out of place. She had eyes only for Elijah, as if her lucky interception during his misadventure had somehow made her responsible for his well-being in perpetuity.

"You were supposed to be with him!" Rebekah finally said, and Lisette slowly raised her head to look at her.

"*You* left before I arrived," Lisette snapped, and Rebekah's cheeks flushed to an even darker scarlet. "He was gone by the time I reached his room. He's not merely sick, Rebekah; Elijah is possessed. He can't be left alone for a moment."

"How convenient for you," Klaus pointed out,

enjoying their bickering. It was as good a distraction as any from what Amalia Giroux had told him. She had bluntly explained Elijah's cure, leaving no room for denial or negotiation. And no matter how many times Klaus turned her words over, looking for another solution, he couldn't find one. No one but Klaus could pay the price of the spell, so Klaus would be forced to sacrifice one of his greatest possessions on his brother's behalf.

Lisette sneered at him, but had no retort to offer. Her fingers wound through Elijah's brown hair, absentmindedly tangling it and then smoothing it again.

Rebekah dropped onto a velvet daybed and ran her hands through her own hair, pulling and arranging it into some semblance of order on top of her head. "So?" she asked, apparently determined to pretend that Lisette had disappeared. "Niklaus, what did the witches have to say for themselves?"

Klaus could almost taste the bitterness the meeting had left in him, and he grimaced in spite of his determination to remain cool-headed. "They laid some fairly steep terms," he began, knowing his siblings would find Amalia's demands just as outrageous as he had. He realized he had taken Amalia's candle from his coat pocket and had been rolling it back and forth between his fingers. He set it down firmly on the table beside him, sat down in a leather chair, and rested his hands on his knees. The group looked at him expectantly. "Before they would tell me how to cure Elijah, they wanted to secure the same portion of the city for themselves as we gave to the werewolves."

"What?" Rebekah all but shouted. "They're to blame for all this! That powder originated with witches in the first place, and it isn't the only thing Tomás has of theirs. He's been building an arsenal of weapons to destroy supernatural beings, and he's been doing it with witches' help. Now they want to use their own treachery as leverage? I hope you slaughtered them."

"It wasn't *these* witches," Elijah sighed. "They may not deserve a third of our city, but they aren't responsible for every renegade out there who uses the same title, either."

"Then who is?" Klaus asked, interested in a new enemy to take out his rage on—there seemed enough of it to go around these days. His fortunes in New Orleans had changed far too quickly for his taste: No matter what he worked to build, circumstances could sweep it all away in a moment. First he had been forced to share his city with the werewolves, and now . . . now he would lose even more. "It's true, though, that they didn't even know for sure that the powder really existed until I told them so," Klaus added, at which

Rebekah rolled her eyes skeptically. "The local clan is out of their depth with Tomás, and so an alliance is as much for their safety as their benefit."

"An alliance," Elijah sighed. "You mean another chunk of our city gone, in exchange for some information? Niklaus, I would never have asked you to agree to that. It may have taken us longer to find a solution on our own, but if the only alternative was giving away another piece of our home, I would have waited."

"I doubt you could have," Lisette muttered, barely seeming to notice anyone else in the room. "I was in your study for hours and hadn't found a single thing of use, and you managed to escape in the meantime."

"All the more reason I should look myself," Elijah argued, although to Klaus, it was all his brother could do to keep his eyes open. "With a little time—"

"Oh, don't be absurd," Rebekah interrupted. "The powder nearly lured you out into the woods earlier, and I doubt that will be the last attempt Tomás makes. The humans have their sights on us and their hooks into you, and time is the one thing we *don't* have. The longer we wait, the higher the risk one of their attacks will hit its mark."

"They won't," Klaus assured her. Elijah could be as noble and long-suffering as he wanted, but it didn't matter: The deal was struck. Whether Klaus liked it or not, the tide in New Orleans was turning against his desires yet again. "While the witches drive a hard bargain, they still did come through with their end of it."

"And now we get to the real cost," Rebekah said. "Magic never gives you anything for free, as we know better than most. So what's it to be this time, Niklaus? What will we be asked to give besides our city?"

"You?" Klaus smirked, tasting bitterness as he did. Rebekah *would* try to play the martyr, when she was the one of the three of them who stood to lose the least. "Nothing of consequence, dear sister, unless you're more attached to that new plaything of yours than I thought. According to Amalia Giroux, Elijah's pain is so intense that it is equal to the pain of one hundred vampires at once. It would kill a hundred normal vampires, but Elijah is strong enough to suffer through that agony for eternity. To offset Elijah's suffering, we have to sacrifice those hundred vampires—an eye for an eye, in a manner of speaking."

Rebekah gasped, and Elijah's brow furrowed deeply.

"A hundred?" Rebekah repeated.

"Amalia gave me that candle," Klaus continued, "and once we light it we have until it burns out to complete the sacrifice. If we succeed in time, Elijah's torment will be extinguished along with the last sputter of the flame."

A silence fell over the room as each of them considered his words. Klaus felt the weight of the task settle more heavily onto his shoulders.

"Niklaus, do we even have so many?" Elijah said, his breath shallow.

"Just above, at my last count," Klaus answered, deliberately avoiding Lisette's steely gray gaze. Lisette had a good head for facts and figures, and she knew what Klaus wouldn't say.

"A hundred and one," she clarified, her voice crisp in the darkened room. "The humans all carry werewolf venom with them now, and they refuse to be turned. We have taken some recent losses, and have not been able to add to our numbers. So excluding the three of you, there were one hundred and one vampires in New Orleans as of last night."

The vast majority of the remaining vampires were Klaus's progeny, the ones he had recently created to form his army. But there were others, like Lisette and that new toy of Rebekah's, and Klaus could see his siblings counting their numbers and recalling each of their names. Lovers, friends, servants, and soldiers: All of them would have to die in order to save Elijah, except for one.

Each of the three Mikaelsons surely had that "one" in mind, but as Klaus looked at Lisette, perched on the bench with his brother's head in her lap, he knew which vampire would be spared. A hundred vampires would have to die at the hands of the Originals, and when it was all said and done, Lisette would be left standing.

It made the prospect of dismantling his army even more painful to Klaus, but there was no point in dwelling. Elijah needed this, and Klaus would be damned if he was going to stand between his brother and a cure.

"I think the witches are lying," Rebekah stated, folding her arms across her chest. "They want us to decimate our own kind to benefit them, and they thought we'd be so desperate to save Elijah that we would fall for their tricks."

Klaus lifted the books that Amalia had given him so that the group could read their titles. "They know us too well, and already followed that train of thought. Here's the evidence they provided," he said. "I've only skimmed it myself, but I've found no reason not to believe what I was told. The only question that remains, as far as I'm concerned, is how we make the most of this unfortunate turn of events. How can we best turn it to our advantage?"

"Advantage?" Lisette repeated, her mouth open in

disbelief. "The deaths of a hundred of your . . . of *us*, and you want to 'make the most' of it?"

"You can't be surprised," Rebekah said. "Our Niklaus doesn't do anything unless it benefits him."

"If we're already doing this," he pointed out, more stung by his sister's accusation than he dared to admit, "why not find a way—"

"We'll see if you really are doing this," Rebekah muttered under her breath, but still clearly enough to be heard.

"Would you care to repeat that?" Klaus asked, his eyes narrowing. "Is there something else you want to say to me, Rebekah?" It was just like her to take a bad situation and make it worse with petty accusations.

"I think you heard exactly what I said," she replied, sitting up and leaning forward. "I think you're looking for a way to turn a hundred murders to your advantage, because if there is no gain for you, you'll find an excuse not to go through with it."

Klaus jumped from his chair, ignoring Elijah's weak protest. "How dare you?" he demanded. "While you were off dallying with that pirate you're so fond of, leaving Lisette to chase down Elijah, I was out there finding a solution to this mess. I went to the witches I despise and gave them a third of our city for our brother, and you dare to suggest I won't give more?"

"I know you, Niklaus," Rebekah spat, not bothering to rise from her seat. "I'm sure you believe you'll do whatever it takes to save Elijah, but I also believe that you'll save yourself first. It's who you are—it's in your blood."

It was a low blow, and they all knew it. Klaus had been raised as a Mikaelson, but he wasn't a full one by birth, and it was perfectly clear which half of his parentage Rebekah thought was to blame for his opportunistic nature. Klaus turned to Elijah, but his brother wouldn't meet his eyes, and that was all Klaus needed to see.

"You can both go to hell," he snapped. "Do what you want with the city and its vampires. If you still don't trust me after all I've done, then Elijah can rot for all I care."

He kicked the chair behind him for emphasis, feeling just the slightest twinge of satisfaction as the leather split and the wood disintegrated. He stalked out of the room, leaving his family to suffer in the cesspool they had made for themselves.

TWENTY-THREE

*R*ebekah sprang up from her daybed, rushing to intercept Klaus before he could leave the mansion. It was so typical of him to storm off, leaving the rest of them to do all the hard work themselves. But Rebekah knew that her life would be much easier if Klaus was on her side. She'd gone too far in the heat of the moment, and she'd found Klaus's weak spot. Once again, the humans had found a way to drive the Mikaelsons apart.

"Don't you dare walk out on me," she ordered, throwing herself between her brother and the wreckage of the shattered front door. "Don't you dare walk out on *him*."

"You don't think I'll lift a finger to help him anyway." Klaus glowered, although he didn't make any move to push his way past her. "You think I'd let Elijah suffer to protect my army. I made them to be *disposable*. That's what soldiers do, Rebekah—they die."

"Perhaps that was unfair of me. But, Niklaus, this catastrophe seems to change its face every hour. I'm feeling buffeted from every side, and—"

"It didn't look like you minded much earlier," Klaus taunted, and for a moment Rebekah felt the movement of the ocean beneath her again. Trust him to notice what she had been up to and then judge her for it. Just because Klaus hadn't managed to love another soul besides his own in the twenty-two years since Vivianne's death didn't make him superior to the lesser beings who eventually moved on from grief.

"That's beside the point," Rebekah answered, grinding her teeth together in frustration. She couldn't even think about Luc, not knowing what was next for him. "None of us is at our best right now, but that's when we need each other the most. You know that's what Elijah would tell us, only he's too weak to come running after you this time. We need to work together, not tear our little family apart."

"Elijah needs his cure, not for us to hold hands and cooperate." Klaus shrugged. He could convey such contempt with that simple gesture that Rebekah nearly slapped him, but more fighting was just the excuse Klaus needed to go off on his own again.

"A hundred vampires will put up a fight," she replied, clenching her fists to keep them by her sides. "Even with the best of intentions, Niklaus, this is not a task for you alone. You've already spent days building new alliances and doling out favors, so why not call in a few of those now? Bring Sampson and your new witch friends into play, and together we can make short work of this disagreeable task. There will be a full moon tonight, and no better time for us all to band together and do what must be done."

"No better time to destroy Tomás and his followers?" Luc asked from the curved staircase, and Rebekah turned a little at the sound of his voice.

"That's the spirit, Luc." Klaus looked up at him, a dangerous gleam in his eye. "We might as well make the most of my army while I still have it."

Luc frowned a little, his blue eyes puzzled, and Rebekah took a deep breath and gave Luc a smile. He hadn't heard enough of the conversation to figure out that her family was about to commit mass murder, and she certainly wasn't about to tell him.

"You said you learned nothing of use during your pursuit of Tomás," she called up to him. "But now you speak of destroying him. Did you think of some clue you had overlooked before?" Rebekah longed to protect him somehow from the fate that awaited him, and she held her breath, hoping that he would be clever enough to demonstrate his usefulness to Klaus. Only one vampire could survive the cure, and as much as Rebekah loved Lisette, she wanted Luc to have a fighting chance as well.

"I said I found nothing but hints and rumors," Luc corrected, descending the rest of the stairs. "But those can be meaningful as well, especially with a little time to put them together."

"Is that what you were doing up there?" Klaus asked, although now he looked more amused than scornful. "I had no idea our Rebekah had taken up with such an intellectual."

"Shut up," Rebekah sighed. "Luc is trying to help, and you can't even be decent enough to listen."

"I have an idea of where the humans might be," Luc went on, ignoring Klaus's dig. He'd been around long enough to know that it was better to let such taunts roll off him—something Lisette had never quite gotten the hang of. Rebekah bit her lip, willing herself to stop comparing the two. "I intended to go investigate myself before bringing the possibility to you, but if you would prefer to go in more force, I feel fairly confident that I'm right."

Before Rebekah could answer, the sound of the protection spell wailed in the walls, signaling the approach of someone toward the house. It could hardly be a vampire in broad daylight, so all three of them turned toward the door, ready to strike at some unexpected enemy.

"What an interesting idea for an entryway," a voice drawled, and Rebekah sized up the newcomer with interest. She was tall and slender, and her only adornment was her waterfall of thick black hair, liberally streaked with white. Klaus's posture relaxed. He seemed to recognize her, and Rebekah gathered that this was the leader of the witches. "Is this the newest fashion in front doors? I'm afraid we haven't quite caught on in the bayou." The woman poked at the splintered wood with one pointy-toed boot.

She couldn't come any farther, even with the door gone. The protection spell would keep her out, Rebekah realized with a certain smug satisfaction. "Can we help you, witch?" she asked, pointedly not inviting her inside.

"You've already done enough for me." The witch smirked, and Klaus's jaw tightened. A third of the city had better be enough, Rebekah agreed silently. Maybe Klaus had been right all along: Maybe New Orleans *wasn't* big enough for three warring supernatural clans. "My name is Amalia Giroux, and I have come to offer *you* help."

"Just like that?" Klaus sounded skeptical, and Rebekah could hear the anger that ran through his voice. "You weren't inclined to offer any favors the last time we met."

"I've traced the provenance of the vinaya vines that your humans cultivated," Amalia explained, ignoring the tension of their meeting. "As we suspected, no witch here had a hand in the trafficking of such dangerous stuff. But we are still not as blameless as I had hoped. Some of my people had dealings with those who traded with Tomás, and a few of them knew more about his scheming than they thought to share with me at the time."

Klaus began to speak, but Amalia cut him off before he could even begin. "I have dealt with my people," she continued firmly. "I will not turn them over to you, or even name them. But harm was done, and I have come in good faith to help you set it right."

"How?" Rebekah asked, genuinely curious. "With vague generalities and a healthy dose of guilt?"

"With warriors," Amalia corrected stiffly. Her

perceptive brown eyes landed on Luc, sizing him up in a way that made Rebekah nervous. "I have an army at my disposal, for . . . whatever it is that you may need destroyed."

Rebekah shifted so that her body blocked the witch's view of her lover. If he had to die, she would see all the others die first. Luc had saved her life, he had seen her true self. Rebekah didn't intend to give him up until she was sure there was no choice left. "An army to lead against the humans, you mean," she suggested.

Klaus made a noise that sounded obnoxiously like a scoff, and Rebekah shot him a glare.

"Tomás has been posing as a merchant," Luc said, ignoring the strange undercurrent of the conversation. He had stayed well back from the door, avoiding the sunlight that spilled in through its empty frame. "I've spent the last few nights trying to find out more about his secrets, but his legitimate pursuits also intrigued me. He has warehouses by the river for his lawful business, and I believe that his followers use one of his buildings for their more rebellious activities."

"That sounds like a reasonable possibility to me," Klaus agreed, his mind catching on to something. Rebekah could tell he hadn't given up on the possibility of coming out of this disaster as the victor—no matter how slim the margins. But how?

"Amalia," Klaus mused, "if your witches helped Tomás amass his collection, might they know where those objects were sent? Surely a merchant—even one leading a double life—would use his own ships and warehouses for those kinds of trades."

"I will find out," Amalia agreed.

"Do it quickly, love, for we must attack tonight," Klaus said. "The full moon won't wait for us, and we will need every advantage against the humans—the werewolves must be in their natural form. The cult of Janus has weapons that can harm each one of us, and together we stand a better chance of overwhelming and destroying them once and for all. When that's done we will deal with Elijah's curse."

Rebekah knew what Klaus wouldn't say in front of Luc: He would let as many vampires die in the battle as necessary to destroy the human threat, before the Originals and their allies turned on the rest. But Klaus seemed too relaxed, too easy, and Rebekah sensed that there was more to his plan than even she understood.

The parlor door opened and Elijah and Lisette stepped out. Elijah leaned heavily on Lisette's shoulder, taking small steps. He gave the witch a nod—he knew who she was. Elijah never stopped governing his city, even in these dire circumstances.

"Are you certain your brother can wait for you to

wage war on the humans?" Amalia said, acknowledging Elijah's entrance, but still speaking to Klaus. It was as if she thought Elijah was too frail to answer for himself, or that his mind had been weakened by the pain he was enduring.

"My brother is right," Elijah answered firmly. "My cure can wait for a few hours or even an entire night, but Tomás and his people can't. I want them out of my city—now."

Rebekah expected Luc to react somehow, to ask what Elijah meant about a cure. But Luc seemed oblivious to the implication of Elijah's words, and he didn't so much as glance toward Rebekah for an explanation.

"You should be resting, Elijah," Rebekah said after a long moment.

"There is still time to rest before the battle tonight," Elijah disagreed, and Rebekah felt her eyes widen as she understood the full extent of his words.

"You're not coming along," she blurted. "You couldn't possibly."

"You may need me," Elijah argued, although it was obvious to everyone that he could barely stand, much less fight.

"At the risk of being indelicate, brother, you may turn on us," Klaus pointed out. "You're not cured yet, and until you are you're a danger to all of us."

"I'll be fine," Elijah insisted, and Lisette bit her lip. She was afraid to argue with him, Rebekah thought uncharitably, afraid to jeopardize her connection to Elijah and, along with it, her life.

Rebekah felt the ball of dread in her stomach continue to grow. No matter what she told herself, she wasn't convinced that Luc would be allowed to live. And if he did, it would only be because Rebekah lost Lisette, who had been a friend to her for decades. Tomás had promised that Rebekah would lose everything, and sure enough, the things she loved kept getting stripped away.

Marguerite was dead and gone—at best, she was only a pawn in this cruel game. Luc and Lisette might not survive to see the end of the night, and Elijah . . . Elijah was going to insist on riding into battle no matter what anyone said to stop him. And that meant Rebekah might lose him, too.

"It's decided, then," Klaus announced, his voice ringing clearly up and down the front hall. "We will meet near the warehouses just after moonrise, and, Amalia, you will lead us to the correct hideout. We'll send word to the werewolves, and Tomás will find three armies at his doorstep tonight."

Amalia curtseyed deeply, although her head remained proudly unbent. "My people will be yours tonight," she agreed, "and then our debt will be paid." She turned on her heel and left without the traditional farewell, leaving the five vampires to stare at her departing back.

"I need a moment with my brothers," Rebekah continued when she was sure the witch couldn't hear. "Lisette, Luc . . . please."

She took Elijah's arm, nodding encouragingly to Lisette. The younger vampire reluctantly let Elijah's weight pass from her shoulders to Rebekah's. Then Lisette smoothed her hair back and hooked her arm through Luc's. "Come," she told him, her voice bright with false cheer. "We'll spread the word to the others and make sure everything is prepared for tonight."

Luc glanced over his shoulder as Lisette led him away, but Rebekah was scared to meet his gaze, troubled at what truths he might find in her eyes. Once he was gone, Rebekah turned to her brothers. "Elijah, the whole point of this desperate scheme is to save your life. Are you really willing to risk it just so you can observe the last battle of a hundred doomed vampires?"

"If they're all going to die for me one way or another, the least I can do is fight with them," Elijah replied calmly. Rebekah could feel his pulse racing through his skin, and up close she could see that his jaw was clenched tightly against the pain. "I won't risk the possibility that Tomás might slip through our fingers because I was in too much pain to stop him. I'm an Original; I'm stronger than that."

"And when the vinaya starts calling to you again like it did last night?" Klaus demanded. He stalked into the drawing room, pulling a small iron key from his pocket as he went.

"Niklaus," Rebekah warned, but he refused to acknowledge her.

Instead, Klaus unlocked the iron box that held the White Oak stake and held it up for Elijah to see. "Don't make us kill you in the middle of all we're doing to save you."

Elijah's dark eyebrows lifted in surprise, and he leaned a bit more heavily on Rebekah's arm. "That's a step up from your silver daggers, brother," he said at last. "I have every confidence that you'll use it if you must."

"He doesn't *want* to!" Rebekah cried, furious at the resigned sound of Elijah's words. She wanted to shake him, but she couldn't bring herself to cause him any further hurt. His suffering had already clouded his thinking—that much was obvious. "Just stay here and let us handle this. We're not children, Elijah. We haven't been for a long time."

For a moment she saw them again as they had been, three children running in the sun. She could feel the heat of the daylight on her skin, hear her brothers' laughing shouts, smell the flowers she wore in her hair. Rebekah had all but died again from the power of that memory, and then she had been reborn from it. She wanted to share that feeling with Elijah, with everyone. The whole of New Orleans deserved the resurrection that Rebekah had experienced. Maybe the battle to come was what they all needed.

"I know you're not children," Elijah sighed. "Believe me. But I can't wait here like a prisoner, wondering all night if I might be able to help. So accept that, Rebekah. If you're as capable as you say, you'll be able to kill me if that's what it comes to. And I don't doubt for a moment that Niklaus will do what is necessary."

Klaus placed the jagged branch back in its box and locked it securely. "We'll decide this tonight, brother," he promised. "If you're still of sound mind at moonrise, you and our stake will come along to enjoy the spectacle."

TWENTY-FOUR

*A*lejandra slipped her silky dress down over one shoulder, then the other. Elijah watched her, entranced, as she revealed a magical expanse of skin. Her breasts gleamed in the moonlight that seemed to come from everywhere at once, and still the gown kept sliding down, down, down toward the floor.

She looked up at him slyly, her green eyes glittering through the web of her black eyelashes, a knowing smile playing on her lips. She knew how he desired her, and she enjoyed seeing it written all over his face. She was teasing him, toying with him, delaying his pleasure until the moment he couldn't stand to wait another second.

Alejandra stepped closer, and Elijah's fist clenched over the White Oak stake in his hand. He wanted her; he wanted her more than anything else. But he knew that was wrong, that there was something out there that was more important than his longing for Alejandra. It wasn't real; *she* wasn't real.

He could feel the warmth of her skin so close to his, and smell the smoke and whiskey in her curled black hair. She certainly seemed real, and although he knew better, Elijah's grip on the stake relaxed a little. Her presence made him feel weak, and her naked body washed white by the full moon held the promise of his restoration.

"I've missed you," he told her, hating himself for the truth of that confession.

"I'm right here." She smiled, and reached down to caress the side of his face, tracing the line of his jaw with one fingernail.

Elijah closed his eyes and drove the stake into her chest, unable to watch as it struck home. He could feel the wood pierce her skin and crack her ribs, then separate the muscle of her heart. She screamed, a high, wailing sound that was echoed by a sudden blast of wind outside.

The windows slammed open and the tempest swirled into the room, and Elijah opened his eyes to see Alejandra's face blazing with fury. Her hair billowed in the rising storm, and her fingers bent like claws, reaching for his throat.

Then she disappeared, melting away into the howling wind, dissolving like poison into wine. She was replaced by pain: burning, searing, miserable pain that threatened to destroy Elijah from the inside out. Without Alejandra, there was no hope for him, the pain whispered. There would never be anything to fill the space where she had been, and Elijah would suffer without her forever.

He couldn't even move anymore, as if his limbs were being pinned down by someone much stronger than himself. He strained his eyes open, returning to the place of his suffering.

As the last of his hallucination slipped away, his agony grew even worse, amplified immeasurably by the thudding of his heart in his chest. His breath seemed to scorch his throat and lungs, and the faint sound of crickets outside the window might as well have been a metal hatchet tapping inside his ear.

Lisette tightened her grip on his forearms, and in spite of himself, Elijah groaned in pain. "You were sleeping," she told him, her voice betraying a concern that bordered on fear.

The sky outside his windows was newly dark,

with only the first scattering of stars piercing the sky. Moonrise was still hours away. The battle hadn't started yet, but Elijah had dreamed through the better part of the day. Thanks to Alejandra's snare, he had almost missed his chance to prove that he was stronger than some magic trick, that he could still fight and kill like an Original.

"It's late," he said, struggling against Lisette's hands. "Rebekah and Niklaus must be at each other's throats from waiting so long. You should have woken me."

"I haven't been able to wake you any more than I've been able to force you to sleep," Lisette said, letting go of his arms at last. She was still between him and the door, he couldn't help but notice, and she didn't look inclined to budge. "But I'll be damned if I'm going to let you walk out of here."

"What do you mean?" Elijah asked, trying to make sense of her total lack of urgency. They needed to be in position, narrowing down the many warehouses by the river until they could surround Tomás's. The wolves needed to be in place by the time the moon rose, and Elijah was slower than he cared to admit at the moment. "There's too much to do before the fight. Lisette, I'm delaying the others when they already need to be in position."

She bit her lip and looked away, and Elijah could

read the entire truth in her face. "Don't worry about all that right now," she suggested. "Please. Just get back into the bed and rest."

"They've gone already," Elijah said, and she flinched a little as his words struck at her secret. "My sister and brother thought it easier to leave me behind than to worry about me in the midst of a battle. They are unsure of my health and unconvinced of my loyalties, and so they set you over me like a guard dog and went off to fight my battle without me."

"They were so worried about you," Lisette soothed, but Elijah was in no mood to hear it.

"I worry about *them*," he reminded her. He finally noticed the silver candle burning beside his bed: It was the one Amalia Giroux had given to Klaus. A hundred vampires needed to die before it burned itself out. "When have my siblings ever been better off without my help? Alejandra and Tomás separated us on purpose, knowing how much weaker we are when we're apart. Did they not consider the stupidity of doing exactly what their enemies had conspired to do?"

"They considered that twelve hours ago, more or less, you were running headlong toward the open forest as if the love of your life waited for you there," Lisette responded, her hurt showing more than she probably wished it would. "That the powder can control you is no fault or weakness of yours, Elijah. It's no reflection on you. It's just the way things are. And as long as you're under its influence, you're a danger to everyone around you, and so they thought it best to let you sleep."

"*They* thought," Elijah repeated, intrigued by her choice of words. "What about you, Lisette? You would never have chosen to stay out of a fight just to watch me dream. You want to be there, in the thick of things, and you can't possibly believe I'm dangerous enough to justify both of us staying home."

She rolled her eyes at his transparent manipulation, but Elijah could also see he had struck on something true. "I told you that I would always be here for you, you idiot," she said. "There will be other wars, Elijah, and other chances to fight. Of *course* I'd rather be in the thick of battle beside you than sitting here, but this is my mission. I will stay with you here until you're cured."

Elijah stepped closer to her, taking in every faint freckle on the bridge of her nose. "I'm already out of bed, though," he pointed out. "And with you along to keep me in line, I might as well be cured."

"How do you expect me to do that?" Lisette demanded, folding her arms across her chest. "You're about a thousand years older than I am, and you're possessed by a dead woman with access to magic I've never even seen. I got lucky once, Elijah, but let's not pretend I'll be any help if things go really wrong."

She was right. But Lisette didn't need to be stronger than he was. She only needed to be armed. "Come with me," Elijah suggested, a bit more softly and with the offer of compromise in his tone. "There's something I need to show you."

He refused to lean on her as they made their way down the staircase and to the drawing room. He had almost grown used to the searing pain that seemed to want to rip his body apart from the inside. It had been intolerable at first, but after days of having no other choice, Elijah was almost able to ignore it.

"What is that?" Lisette asked when he had forced open the iron box and pulled out the White Oak stake for her to see. She touched it curiously, running her fingers along the rough bark. Elijah shuddered to see her so casual with it, but any stake could destroy a vampire like Lisette. She had no particular reason to dread this one any more than all the rest.

"This is the weapon that can kill me," Elijah explained, folding her palm around the stake and releasing it into her care. "Bring it with you, and be ready to use it if you must."

Lisette stared at the stake as if seeing it for the first time, then she looked back up at Elijah, momentarily speechless. "I can't use this," she whispered at last. "Elijah, I would never be able to use this on you."

"You can and you will," he assured her. "I have no doubts, Lisette. You have proved that I can trust you with my life, and I know I can trust you with my death. Whether you need to use this or whether you don't, you will not make a mistake."

Lisette opened her mouth again and then closed it, apparently thinking better of her reply. A wolf howled somewhere out in the bayou—a real one, as the full moon was still nearly an hour from rising. But that time would be wasted if they didn't hurry.

The doorframe was still an empty hole leading out into the darkness. Elijah stepped through and Lisette followed, tucking the stake into the bodice of her dress as she went.

Elijah smelled the powder just a moment before the pain began again in earnest. It smelled a little sweet and somehow spicy, like the perfume of some exotic land he couldn't quite place. Lisette cried out and then went perfectly still, and he knew that the substance had worked its way into her lungs as well.

Tomás stepped up onto veranda, his dark cloak swirling around him like a second shadow. A silver clasp glittered at his throat, and Elijah could make out the shape of a head with two faces, each looking in opposite directions. One faced the future and the other the past, he remembered dimly: Janus, the twins.

"How good of you to come out," Tomás greeted the two vampires. His pale green eyes flickered between the two of them, sizing up Lisette in a way Elijah found deeply distasteful. "I hope you don't mind that I took advantage of that witch's arrival to cross your protection spell unannounced."

Elijah tried to answer, but his mouth no longer belonged to him. Tomás reached out to stroke Lisette's flame-colored hair as if he were appraising merchandise. "I'm glad you weren't left alone," he said to Elijah, although his eyes still lingered on Lisette. "I have work to do in this house, and you and this beautiful woman here are going to help me."

TWENTY-FIVE

*K*laus's army, a restless, shifting mass of violence and hunger, was gathered on the docks
that ran along the Mississippi River. Klaus counted
his soldiers, making sure that every last vampire had
answered his call. Elijah's health depended on their
obedience.

Klaus could see Rebekah scanning the crowd as
well, her full mouth set in a serious line. To his pleasant
surprise, his sister had readily agreed to his true plan,
once he had explained the extent of it to her. The
insidious corruption of New Orleans's residents had
seeped into the very bones of the city, and she felt as
strongly as Klaus did that their only choice was to start

over and wipe the slate clean. This would be more than just another battle: It would be a new beginning.

The solution to nearly all their problems lay on the other side of the warehouse door behind Klaus. The storeroom was vacant for now—the werewolves' scouts had confirmed that the whole neighborhood was empty, actually, except for the supernatural beings. But it wouldn't stay that way for long. Klaus gave the doors a solid bang with his fist to get everyone's attention. When his soldiers were silent Klaus cleared his throat.

"This is where we will stalk our prey," Klaus announced, and his voice echoed off the water. "The loathsome rats we have come to exterminate call this place home." Amalia had been as good as her word. Her witches had located Tomás's warehouse, a huge wooden building just beside the river. They were waiting a bit farther upstream, ready to join the vampires and werewolves in destroying the Cult of Janus, but unaware of what else Klaus had in mind.

He reached behind his back to thrust the double doors open, revealing the interior of the warehouse behind him. The seemingly endless room was full of half-burnt candles, scraps of parchment, and cast-off clothing, sure signs that Tomás's friends had been using this as a meeting place. There were also plenty of crates and boxes stacked along the walls, and based on

Klaus's earlier scouting, it appeared that business was good. If Tomás had been as talented a rebel as he was a merchant, New Orleans might belong to him by now. He had already seen that the warehouse was packed with silks and tea from China, cinnamon from Dutch Ceylon, Ottoman fine leather, and truly impressive quantities of Barbados rum.

"The humans meet here at midnight on the full, new, and half moons," Klaus went on, stepping back to let his vampires inside. "They will come tonight and gather here to plot their next move against us. And we'll already be here, waiting for them. Won't that be a nice surprise?"

A cheer went up from the soldiers, and Klaus added his own shout. He wanted them in good spirits, liquored up and ready to fight without asking too many questions. Enthusiasm was the only ally he needed, and his army had that in spades.

Klaus loosened a few crates of the rum and pried them open while his army filled the warehouse. He tossed a bottle to José, then pulled out another. The black-haired thief popped off the cork and took a long pull before passing the bottle to a former whore. She drank so eagerly that a few drops ran down her face and spilled on the dirty floor.

Klaus smiled to himself and continued passing out

the rum, whipping his soldiers into a frenzy of chaos and pandemonium. "All we have to do is wait," he shouted, and this time the roar that answered him was almost deafening.

Rebekah pushed her way through the crowd of wild and rowdy vampires. "My dear sister," Klaus announced, feeling expansive so near to his moment of triumph. "Total victory is nearly at hand. Drink with us."

Klaus pulled the last flask from the crate and bit off the top of the bottle, spilling it liberally as he handed it to Rebekah. She wrinkled her snub nose in disgust, but she drank from it all the same before pouring the rest out on the ground. Klaus tore open the next crate.

"Luc came back during that stirring speech of yours," she told him, then snarled viciously at a vampire who had the poor judgment to bump into her shoulder. "He says the werewolves are getting restless this close to moonrise. Sampson has them waiting downriver, so that he and Amalia can close in from opposite directions once the humans are inside. No one will escape."

"Neither friends nor enemies nor innocent bystanders," Klaus agreed, restless for the beginning of the bloodbath.

"We have no friends, Klaus," Rebekah replied, "and no one here is innocent. We only have enemies."

"Every time we turn to the witches or the werewolves

for help, it only strengthens them," Klaus agreed. "They profit whenever someone moves against us, and it's time to be done with them. Even if it requires a sacrifice."

New Orleans would burn, and whatever was left in the morning would be a reborn world.

"One hundred vampires, with Luc as the hundredth," Rebekah mused. "Not to mention anyone else who showed the poor judgment to get involved in all of this."

"It's the only way we can take control of our own destiny," he replied, his eyes wandering around the room again, making sure all was in order.

Klaus was impressed by Rebekah's commitment to her word. When she'd suggested that Luc could act as a messenger between the three armies, Klaus had been sure it was only a pretext to keep her lover out of harm's way.

But one hundred vampires needed to die that night, and when Elijah failed to wake at sunset, Luc's fate had been sealed. There was no one better to keep watch over Elijah than Lisette, and Rebekah had apparently made her peace with that. Klaus had never thought much of Rebekah's tiresome obsession with love, but he was glad to see that at least her brother's life mattered more to her than some blond pirate she had met a mere month ago.

That was the difference between her and Klaus: Rebekah always had hope for the next great love she believed was waiting around the corner for her. Klaus had lost that hope decades ago. There was no more life-changing, earth-moving love out there for him, and that left only power.

The werewolves and the witches wanted to take that from him, but Klaus wouldn't give them the satisfaction. He had seen more of the world than any of them would ever see, and he understood it far better than they ever could. To them, "power" meant a place in New Orleans, but by the time *he* was done, there would be nothing left of New Orleans, and no one left to fight over it. That would suit Klaus just fine.

"Drink!" he shouted, and bottles were raised in the air all across the warehouse. Klaus could smell the heavy liquor permeating the windowless room; the place was filling with it.

"They'll be stumbling fools by the time the humans get here," Rebekah said. "Tomás isn't going to walk into a trap laid by a bunch of drunks."

"We want them drunk," Klaus disagreed, "but my soldiers will fall into line when the time comes." His warriors were loyal to him; they practically revered him. It would be a terrible blow to lose his legion, but at least he could ensure that the entire city would share in his loss. If Klaus couldn't have his army, than no one else in New Orleans would have one, either. "Keep them drinking."

Klaus elbowed his way through the sea of carousing vampires and made his way toward the door. As he stepped through, he was surprised to see Luc heading away from the warehouse with his hands shielding his face and his head bowed.

"Benoit!" Klaus called, and Luc startled and turned. "Go back in to my sister and enjoy the celebration while it lasts. I'll keep an eye out for any messengers. We'll have plenty of warning when the humans are on their way."

Luc glanced at the door of the warehouse, looking tempted by the raucous laughter within. "I promised Sampson I would give him one last report before moonrise," he explained. "Once the wolves transform, communication will be effectively cut off."

"That sounds like Sampson's problem, not mine." Klaus shrugged. "The werewolves know where we are, and they know when to close in. If they need more coddling than that, they're in the wrong war."

"Agreed." Luc hesitated for one last moment, as if he was trying to think of more to say, but Klaus only watched him steadily. "Well, then," the vampire said. "Back to the celebration it is."

He strolled toward the warehouse door, and Klaus began his prowl around the shipping district that sprawled along the river. The March night was dark and empty, a shock to his senses after the festivities inside the warehouse. But he began to pick up the telltale signs of life around him: footsteps along the wharf, horses whickering in a nearby stable, and the shifting of warm bodies in the cold night air. A steady breeze danced among the warehouses, and Klaus could see some quick-moving clouds on the horizon, promising that a strong wind was on its way. Perfect.

Klaus moved carefully along an unpaved street, alert for signs of the three armies that would soon converge on the warehouse. He could smell the smoke of torches drifting downstream on the wind—those must belong to the witches. The werewolves wouldn't burden themselves with such things so close to moonrise, and the humans still thought they were meeting in secret. Klaus could already see the bright haze where the moon would soon edge into the sky. He stayed alert for the first howl, the confirmation that Sampson's pack had begun to change.

Then, at last, Klaus heard the muted footsteps of a human coming his way. There was another person in the next alley over, and a third slyly approaching from the wharf.

It was all about to begin, and Klaus breathed in the sweet smell of his coming victory.

Klaus ran silently for the warehouse, crossing the distance of a dozen city blocks in the blink of an eye. He only had a few minutes to shut down the liquor-fueled party before Tomás's foot soldiers got close enough to notice.

"Silence!" he roared as he closed the warehouse doors behind him, and the drunken vampires did their best to obey. "The humans are approaching," he went on more quietly. "We want them all inside before they realize we're here. No one flees, no one escapes."

His vampires dispersed like a flock of starlings, fitting into hiding places above and behind the crates that ringed the walls. They took their empty rum bottles with them, but the floor was already well-saturated with the liquor. The humans would notice the smell, but there was a world of difference between the stench of spilled liquor and the sight of a hundred drunken vampires.

The first of the cultists cracked the doors open just enough to creep inside, wary of the cloying darkness that greeted him. He stopped on the threshold, his nostrils flaring a little, then another conspirator paused behind him.

"Don't light your lantern yet," the first one whispered. "Do you smell that?"

"Did one of those cases of rum get knocked down?" the second one muttered, sounding more irritated than afraid. "I told the boy not to stack them that way, but of course he didn't listen."

"I'll be sure to beat him in the morning," another voice drawled sarcastically. Klaus heard a match strike against wood, and then a lantern popped and sizzled to life. "It's just on the floor," the man went on. "You won't burn to death just because I'm holding a lantern all the way up here."

The glow from the flame he had lit grew steadily, illuminating each new arrival. There had to be several hundred of them, and the warehouse soon filled with their voices and warmth. Klaus could hardly believe that none of them had noticed that they were surrounded, but he was sure his luck wouldn't hold for much longer. He had never intended to start without Tomás, but he was starting to worry that there might be no choice. *Hold . . . hold . . .* he thought silently to his vampires, hoping that none of them would give away their position before the cult's ringleader arrived.

"What's that?" one of the humans asked suddenly, staring raptly into the shadows of the northern wall.

"Attack!" Klaus bellowed, unable to risk another second's delay.

Vampires sprang from everywhere at once, and the humans in the center of the room screamed and collided with one another in their panic. Klaus positioned himself beside the door, ready to kill anyone who approached it from the inside but still hoping against hope that Tomás might come running to his friends' aid.

A dozen of them were killed immediately in the first onslaught, but the rest quickly organized themselves. As Klaus had suspected, they had not come unarmed, and he saw at least three vampires go down writhing in the grip of some kind of otherworldly smoke.

A human threw an amulet onto the alcohol-soaked floor, and sparks rose up out of it, swirling and coalescing into the glittering shape of a dragon. Klaus stared at it, impressed in spite of himself, as it roared, snapped its jaws, and beheaded one of his soldiers where she stood. A vampire reached a hawk-nosed woman and sank his fangs into her throat, only to reel back, gasping and spitting as if he had been poisoned.

The humans were putting up a good fight, especially considering they were without their leader. "Where the hell is he?" Rebekah demanded, catching Klaus by his arm. "Your idiot vampires gave themselves away too soon."

"Amalia and Sampson will be driving any stragglers here," Klaus reminded her. "If he's nearby, they'll bring him in."

The door burst open almost before he had finished speaking, and Amalia Giroux stood framed in the moonlight outside. Her black hair and dark red gown billowed around her in the rising wind, and the nearest humans fell back just at the sight of her. The sound of a vicious wolf's howl followed behind her: Klaus's final guests had arrived at last.

Werewolves sprang through the open door, led by a massive, muscular beast with a distinctive lantern jaw who could only be Sampson Collado. More witches eased their way in behind the wolves, casting their torches aside with a carelessness that made Klaus wince. He had made the warehouse into a tinderbox, and he had no intention of being inside when he decided it was time to set it on fire.

Klaus grabbed a young witch by the collar of his frock coat and spun him around. "Did you find Tomás on your way here?" he asked. The witch flinched away from the expression on Klaus's face and shook his head mutely.

"It's not like we can ask the wolves," Rebekah fumed. "But it doesn't matter. Niklaus, he would never let himself get caught up in this. He's too smart for this.

Tomás has been a step ahead of us the entire time, and now he'll slip through our fingers once again."

A werewolf fell to the floor, writhing and whimpering in a net of woven purple wolfsbane the humans had produced, seemingly from nowhere. A few people were struggling to open some of the crates, and Klaus realized that he had laid his ambush squarely in the middle of the Cult of Janus's armory. Every weapon Tomás had spent his life amassing was here, and yet he had apparently just walked away. The only way he could leave such treasures behind was if there was something more alluring in his sights.

"Perhaps he had a more pressing matter to deal with," Klaus reasoned, half to himself. "Or perhaps he got wind of our attack."

"A more pressing matter," Rebekah repeated, watching as two vampires tore a human in half between them. "What could be—?"

Klaus realized it at the same moment as Rebekah, and the two of them stared at each other in horror. "Elijah," he said. "Tomás knew we would be here, and Elijah would be all but unguarded."

"We haven't cured him yet," Rebekah said, taking in the massacre of the battle before her. "If we go now, we may lose our chance."

"You go," Klaus told her, opening the door wide enough for her to pass. "I'll stay here and clean up."

Rebekah turned to leave, then froze. "Damn it," she muttered to herself, then wheeled back to face Klaus. "Tomás isn't here, but Niklaus: I haven't seen Luc, either. Not since before you went out to watch for the humans. I don't know where he is."

Klaus's memory recalled everything in complete detail. He could see the range of troubled expressions that had crossed Luc's face during their brief conversation, and he could count the steps the bandit had taken toward the warehouse. But Klaus had turned away before Luc had made it all the way to the doors and slipped inside. He'd been too focused on the bigger picture, and had underestimated the will of a single vampire. Of all people, he wasn't going to let Luc be the one who let his plan come crumbling down.

Klaus could see his own emotion magnified on his sister's face as they both registered the betrayal of a man they'd assumed to be harmless. Rebekah had always had horrible taste in men, and she couldn't help but make the same mistakes over and over again. If only she wouldn't drag the rest of her family down with her.

"We'll track him down, too," Klaus promised, although in his mind he could see the slender silver taper by Elijah's bed, melting away into nothing before they had finished the sacrifice. If they failed, they wouldn't get another chance, and Elijah would be trapped like this forever.

Amalia had been unable or unwilling to tell him how long the candle would take to burn, but from its size, it couldn't possibly last until sunrise. In a few hours it would be gone, and ninety-nine vampires would have died for nothing . . . unless Lisette took Luc's place and died for Elijah. Would she be prepared to sacrifice herself for him? It seemed like the answer would be yes, but some part of Klaus hated to cause his brother that further pain.

"Rebekah, one way or another, all of this will end tonight. Go to Elijah, and kill anyone or anything that gets in your way."

Rebekah fled, and for a moment Klaus almost pitied Luc. If his sister did happen to find him first, she would happily rip him limb from limb. Then a witch screamed, a high, unearthly sound, and Klaus was jolted back to the matter at hand.

Death was everywhere in the warehouse, but there needed to be more. Even four armies clashing in an enclosed space would eventually have survivors, and Klaus didn't intend for anyone to leave this battle alive.

He stepped outside and bolted the doors shut, trapping them all inside. He had intended to stay outside with Rebekah and ensure that no one escaped the doomed building, but it didn't matter. In the chaos of combat no one would notice that they were locked inside, not until it was too late. The warehouse was a well-laid death trap, and Klaus didn't need to watch it spring to be sure of that.

A few of the torches the witches had brought with them still smoldered on the dirt of the unpaved street, and Klaus picked one up and touched it to the wood of the warehouse's outside wall. When the flames caught he used another torch to light the next section of wall, then moved along the length of the warehouse, methodically lighting it piece by piece.

The fire eagerly consumed the seasoned wood of the warehouse, and Klaus paused to enjoy his handiwork for a few more moments. Vampires, humans, witches, and werewolves alike would perish in the inferno that was just beginning to burn, and they would take all of Klaus's problems with them. If Klaus had to lose his army, to give up his dreams of conquest, then the entire city would share in his loss.

He carried the last few torches to the neighboring warehouses, setting one fire after another in the rising wind. There would be nowhere to run, even if anyone managed to get through the burning walls and bolted doors. As far as Niklaus Mikaelson was concerned, New Orleans was over.

The fire spread quickly, devouring the buildings before his eyes, and Klaus wondered why he hadn't thought of burning down the whole city years ago. When he caught Tomás, he'd have to thank him for the marvelous inspiration.

TWENTY-SIX

*T*he fire was spreading nearly as fast as Rebekah could run. The wind that whipped along the river carried it from one building to the next, allowing it to grow out of control. It leaped from the treasury to swallow a church, engulfing every house in its path. By the time the citizens woke to the threat, the inferno would be well beyond their ability to contain it. This was the morning of one of their holy days, Rebekah remembered dimly, and she hoped they would appreciate their own opportunity for resurrection.

She wondered if Elijah could feel it as the vampires trapped inside the warehouse died one by one, whether each death brought him closer to his old self. Could he sense the sacrifice even as it was happening? Did he know his siblings had decided to condemn the entire city along with its vampires?

Rebekah had let herself be caught up in Klaus's poetry of a clean slate, of a New Orleans forced to rise from its own ashes, but there could be no fresh start if Tomás was still on the loose, no cure for Elijah with Luc unaccounted for, and no peace for the Mikaelsons until every bit of the old city had been burned away. Klaus had orchestrated a spectacular fire, but there was still much work to be done.

Rebekah heard shouts and a few screams behind her, and she knew that the city was waking to its fate at last. They would form brigades to bring water from the river, and they would fight valiantly for their home— just like the Mikaelsons had always done, and like Tomás believed he was doing. Rebekah knew better than anyone how impossible it was to hold on to a home . . . and how unthinkable it was to give one up.

Rebekah could hear her heart pounding as she approached the mansion. She and Klaus had abandoned Elijah with only one guard, leading the bulk of their army to their deaths. And Tomás didn't care how many of his followers died, not if it meant he got to the Originals. He couldn't have planned it any better if he had tried.

The Mikaelsons' mansion looked cold and unwelcoming, and Rebekah could sense that something was wrong inside as soon as it was in view. For more than sixty years, the house had belonged to her, Klaus, and Elijah, but there was something unfamiliar about it now. She knew that the powerful protection spell Ysabelle Dalliencourt had worked all those years ago made the house indestructible, but Tomás had once promised to destroy *everything* Rebekah loved. She loved that house, and had left her brother and her best friend behind the supposed safety of its walls.

She half expected the protection spell to stop her at the door, but she felt nothing as she charged inside. Any other supernatural being besides the three Originals would have required an invitation, but if a human like Tomás had managed to cross onto their land undetected, he could have walked right inside. Rebekah thought she could smell him in the air of the front hall: the lingering odor of smoke and vinaya and mortality.

She started up the grand staircase, toward Elijah's room and the end of the little candle that still burned there, but the soft scrape of a shoe against marble froze her in her tracks.

"Rebekah," Luc whispered, and she spun. He stood in the hall, looking every bit as surprised as she was. "Thank God you've come."

"Where have you been?" she demanded, lowering her voice to match his. "What the hell are you doing *here*?"

"I went out to make one last report to the werewolves," Luc explained hurriedly, his eyes flickering up the staircase behind her. "Some of them thought the humans were approaching already, but Sampson said it was too early. I got curious and found fresh boot prints, and they led me here. I think Tomás saw the ambush and escaped, but I couldn't risk approaching him if he has some of that powder left."

"I clearly remember ordering you to go back into the warehouse," Klaus announced from the gaping space where the front door had been, and Luc paled at the sight of Rebekah's brother. He was suddenly caught between two Original vampires, and Rebekah could imagine that was an uncomfortable place to be.

"Tomás is here, and he may already have Elijah," Rebekah said to them both. There was no point in arguing among themselves when the real enemy was in their own house. "Stop quarreling and help me look."

"They have to be upstairs somewhere," Luc said. "I've been making a circuit of the staircases in case Tomás tried to take your brother away, but no one has come down since I got here."

"How useful of you," Klaus grumbled. Rebekah

could hear imminent violence in his voice, but he only pushed past Luc to join Rebekah on the steps. Her brother's cold-blooded cynicism cut both ways. As long as Tomás was unaccounted for, Klaus would be content to use Luc to defeat him. And then he would destroy Luc without a second thought . . . unless Lisette managed to get herself killed first. Rebekah barely knew what to hope for anymore. "I saw some candlelight in the attic from outside, and there's no reason for anyone to be there."

Klaus and Rebekah ran up the stairs together, and she could hear Luc trailing behind them. There was a tapestry at the end of the hall, with a melodramatic maiden and a weeping unicorn—a sentimental piece of work that Rebekah had chosen for the certainty that it would irritate Klaus. It concealed a humble wooden door that led to the attic, where he liked to paint and brood, and to Rebekah's keen eye the tapestry was already a little askew.

Klaus led the way, silently signaling which parts of the creaky old steps to avoid. The attic above was eerily quiet, with nothing to mask the sound of their approach, but Rebekah could feel Tomás in front of her.

Klaus opened the door, and the three of them stepped into the attic.

Tomás held a knife that glittered in the candlelight, and Rebekah could see a long, vertical cut on each of Elijah's forearms. Lisette held a chalice to catch the blood that dripped from them, careful not to spill a drop. Dozens of Klaus's paintings ringed the sloping walls, creating an unnerving backdrop for the scene. Rebekah knew a ritual when she saw one, and her heart beat faster in her chest.

Tomás turned at the sight of them, smiling pleasantly. "Welcome," he said, drawing a blood-soaked amulet from the chalice and placing it around his own neck. "You're just in time to see your home destroyed."

"This house will still be standing long after the flesh has rotted off your bones," Rebekah told him. "It's too late to save your own life, Tomás, but if you release my brother and Lisette right now, I'll make sure to give you a quicker death than your sister got."

"I don't think so, my dear."

An invisible, soundless *something* surrounded Rebekah. She felt the air sucked out of her lungs, like she was trapped in the middle of a lightning storm. Then with one loud crack, the feeling was gone and the pressure in the room returned to normal. She had no idea what Tomás had just done, but it couldn't be good.

Only after taking a shaky breath did she risk looking at Elijah, who showed no sign of interest or fear. He simply watched Tomás, waiting for his next orders, completely ensnared once again by the vinaya powder. Rebekah couldn't bear the sight of him and Lisette so unlike their usual, powerful selves. Tomás had already brought him so much pain.

Tomás only smirked at Rebekah. "Your time is over, monsters," he said. "The protection spell that you've hidden behind for so long is gone, and now you are exposed to the world."

"That's not possible," Klaus scoffed, circling sideways with his eyes on Elijah. "That spell has held for decades, and you're hardly the first to take a run at it."

"How many of the others were inside the house?" Tomás asked, and Rebekah knew that he was telling the truth. Tomás had yet to make an empty threat, and besides, she had *felt* the spell collapse in on itself. She had known what the sensation was, even though she hadn't been able to put it into words. That change in the air had felt like vulnerability, like fear.

Before any of them managed a reply, Tomás turned to Lisette. "Kill them," he ordered.

Rebekah had just enough time to wonder why he had spoken to her and not Elijah before Lisette's body crashed into her own, slamming her back against the doorjamb so hard that Rebekah felt her spine crack in two.

Luc threw his burly arm around Lisette's throat and dragged her backward, giving Rebekah the spare moment she needed for her back to repair itself. Klaus lunged past her, his turquoise eyes riveted on Tomás.

Elijah intercepted him, and Rebekah watched in horror as Elijah threw Klaus through one of the tall windows that ringed the attic. Its glass shattered into thousands of pieces, and Klaus vanished into the smoky night. Rebekah, able to move again, blocked Elijah's arm before he had a chance to behead Luc.

Elijah *wanted* to kill her, Rebekah realized as his burning stare turned her way. He didn't need to be ordered to, because Alejandra's vinaya powder had poisoned him to the point that he wasn't even her brother anymore. And the cure hadn't worked yet, not with one of the one hundred vampires still left alive.

Luc and Lisette rolled around on the floor, neither able to get the upper hand. Luc was stronger, but Lisette was possessed by a greater desire to win. Cursing her own hesitation, Rebekah hoped that one of them would just kill the other and spare her from having to make the choice.

Tomás edged toward the sloping walls, watching the fight while slowly distancing himself from the vampires. When he saw Rebekah watching him, he spun his cloak and flung some of his deadly powder into her face.

Rebekah ducked, but it was too late. Luc had seen the motion as well, and he rolled and twisted so that Lisette's face came up between Rebekah and Tomás at the last instant, and she inhaled all of the vinaya. Lisette coughed and gasped and then screamed, digging at her eyes until Rebekah saw them bleed.

"Let them go, you son of a bitch!" Rebekah shouted, unsure if Tomás even had the power to undo what he had done to her brother and her friend. "You can have the city if you want it so badly, but I won't let you take Elijah!"

"It was the humans' city first," Tomás snarled, clutching something unseen in one hand that caused Rebekah to hang back warily. "Alejandra and I were happy here, until our father disappeared one night and our mother had to return to a life of indentured servitude to pay off his debts. She came home dirty and exhausted when she was able to come home at all, and no one was brave enough to help us try to seek justice, or even learn what had become of our *papá*."

"Anything might have happened to him," Rebekah pointed out coldly. "In spite of our best efforts to establish order, New Orleans has always been a dangerous place."

"You are the danger!" Tomás screamed, veins standing out from his neck in his attempt to make her understand his suffering. "One of you killed my father, and that one right there"—his hand shot out at Klaus, who had just returned—"killed my twin sister."

Tomás released the object he had been holding and let it fly. The object—a little sphere of metal Rebekah didn't recognize—struck Klaus squarely in the chest, and he reeled back, stunned. His body crashed against one of the large canvases, and Rebekah cursed Tomás's endless supply of tricks.

Try as she might, she couldn't get close to him again. Elijah blocked her, swinging at her head and tripping her up as she tried to dodge away. She lashed out with both legs, tangling them with Elijah's ankles and bringing him to the floor with her. "You don't have to do this," she whispered, and she thought she saw a fleeting expression cross his face. It was a look of unbearable torment, and the sight of it made Rebekah furious for him. No matter what wrongs Tomás believed had been committed against his family in the past, it was no excuse to torture someone like this.

"Elijah, we're trying to help you," Klaus called out as he stumbled to his feet.

"You've done enough to me already," he hissed, and Rebekah grabbed his hands and held them, trying desperately to communicate how much she loved him.

Lisette broke free from Luc and kicked Rebekah

squarely in the face, knocking her away from Elijah and shattering her cheekbone in the process. Klaus, shaking off whatever talisman Tomás had thrown at him, grabbed Lisette's arm and twisted it so far up behind her back that everyone in the room could hear it splinter.

Rebekah lurched to her feet, shaking her head to clear away the red stars that seemed to blossom everywhere she looked. Tomás was carving symbols into the rafters with a knife, driving traces of Elijah's blood into the very fabric of their home. He worked quickly, almost scribbling the runes in order to finish whatever he was doing before he was swept up in the fighting again. All Rebekah needed to do was reach him, and she could put an end to all of this. Tomás was only mortal, and no matter what tricks he had, he would still die like a human.

Tomás reached for the pouch at his belt as he saw her approach, but Luc stumbled backward against him, reeling from a blow by Lisette, and knocked Tomás off balance. Tomás still parried Rebekah's first blow even as he fell back against the rafters, and he clawed at his belt again for the powder that would render Rebekah helpless against him.

But the pouch was gone, and his green eyes widened in fear and understanding as Rebekah caught him by the throat and lifted him, pressing him up against the wall and holding him there. "This isn't the end," he croaked. "You will never be safe."

"I don't need to be safe," Rebekah told him grimly. "I am a Mikaelson."

She pressed against his windpipe, savoring her ability to stop his endless stream of threats at last. Tomás's hand scratched at the designs he had cut into the wood of the rafters, no doubt trying to accomplish one final piece of destruction before he died.

Rebekah squeezed harder, forcing the life out of his pale green eyes. Tomás died silently, and Rebekah hoped that whatever he had left unfinished in the mansion would haunt him for the rest of eternity. She let his limp body drop to the floor and took in her first full breath in weeks. Their meeting at the White Oak tree seemed almost a lifetime ago, and in some ways, it was.

Rebekah turned to Luc, who held the little pouch of vinaya powder in one hand, weighing it with an uncharacteristic thoughtfulness in his twinkling blue eyes. "That was well done," she told him. "Even I didn't see you take it."

"We'll burn that," Klaus decided, holding out his hand for the pouch. "It's too dangerous to exist, even in our hands."

"*Our* hands?" Luc repeated, looking down at the pouch in his palm. Rebekah stepped closer to him, an uneasy feeling in the pit of her stomach. When Luc turned toward her, she froze in place. "The powder is in *my* hands," he corrected. "And so is this."

Carefully, watching Klaus and Rebekah as he did it, Luc bent down and pulled the White Oak stake from its hiding place in his boot. Rebekah gasped and covered her mouth with her hands in shock.

In just a matter of minutes, Luc—her simple, straightforward, easygoing Luc—had managed to obtain vinaya powder from Tomás and the White Oak stake that Lisette must have been carrying for Elijah.

Lisette didn't even seem to notice the stake was gone. She crouched on the floor, holding her head in her hands as if it might split in two. Rebekah remembered how lost and broken Elijah had seemed after Alejandra had been killed—*a puppet with its strings cut*, Alejandra had said. She suspected that Lisette might be experiencing something similar, but one way or another her suffering was almost over. Elijah himself looked no better off, standing still and purposeless behind Lisette, as if his entire reason for living had ended with Tomás's death.

"I knew you were up to no good," Klaus muttered. "Rebekah has the worst taste in men."

Rebekah couldn't even spare the time to be offended. It was true, even if this was a particularly sensitive moment for Klaus to bring it up. Klaus's eyes shifted toward her, trying to signal for a coordinated attack, but Rebekah gave him a tiny shake of her head, hoping that he wouldn't do anything rash. Both of Luc's weapons could mean the end of either one of them, and Elijah, if they made a misstep now. They didn't have another hundred vampires to kill, and there weren't any witches left to make another silver candle. If Luc or Lisette got away, all hope was lost.

"What are you doing, Luc?" she asked, as calmly as she could force her voice to sound. "Sweetheart, put those things down now."

"Why would I put them down?" Luc asked, turning the stake in his hand as if he was testing for the perfect grip. "With these things, I can create my own destiny."

"You found Tomás after we left Mystic Falls," Rebekah realized. "Those times I didn't know where you were, you were meeting with him."

"That's how Tomás was able to stay ahead of our movements," Klaus added, and Rebekah could hear raw murder in his voice. "You even betrayed the secrets of our house's protection spell."

"Whatever he promised you, Luc, you can see that

he won't be able to deliver on it now." Rebekah forced herself to sound soft, understanding, even though all she wanted to do was rip his heart out.

"He had nothing to offer me except the truth." Luc shrugged, glancing with some disgust at Tomás's limp corpse. "All I've wanted my entire life was freedom. I thought that was what you were offering me when you turned me, but that turned out to be a lie. You three have more power than anyone ever should. You control and compel the rest of us to obey your every whim— even you, Rebekah, when it suits you."

"Tomás controlled you," Rebekah whispered. "He used that powder in your hand and made you try to kill me."

"And yet you lived," Luc pointed out, "and you trusted me more than ever. Tomás saw the advantage in that, and so did I."

Klaus caught Rebekah's eye again, and she clenched her fists until her nails dug into her palms. Somewhere on the floor below them, the silver candle was burning low. They couldn't afford to stand around talking all night. If Luc wouldn't give up his weapons willingly— and it was becoming increasingly clear he would not— they were just going to have to take the risk and attack.

Then Lisette stirred and moaned, and Elijah jerked forward at the sound. "Let her go," he growled, lurching unsteadily toward Luc. Rebekah stared at him, amazed by his strength. He was still possessed, still tortured, yet Lisette's suffering drove him to reclaim some control over his mind and body. "I'll shove that powder down your throat and make you choke on it."

He didn't notice the stake, not even when Luc aimed it at Elijah's heart. Rebekah could see her real brother in Elijah's brown eyes, and realized that the powder Tomás used on him and Lisette must be wearing off at last. But too slowly, too unsteadily, and it showed in her brother's every movement.

"Elijah!" Rebekah shouted, throwing herself forward to intercept him. She was too far away, and so was Klaus, yet she knew Elijah couldn't hope to overpower Luc without their help.

As Rebekah watched, sick with fear, Elijah lurched and then hesitated at exactly the wrong moment, leaving his chest unprotected for Luc's strike. Rebekah dove forward, trying to cover the last of the distance between them by sheer force of will, but Lisette was closer. With a last, desperate scream, the young vampire rose to her feet, placing herself directly between Elijah's heart and the White Oak stake in Luc's hand.

It plunged into her chest with a sickeningly wet noise, piercing her flesh as easily as if it had been silk. Lisette's clear gray eyes widened for a moment, staring at Luc in surprise. He hesitated, shocked by the sight of the stake protruding from her chest instead of his target's.

Elijah collapsed to the floor, unconscious. The cure was working, Rebekah realized through the haze of the moment. Lisette's death must have triggered it, although there was no telling how long his healing would take. Rebekah wanted to run to him, to cradle his dark-haired head in her lap and watch the witches' spell do its work. But she couldn't quite yet—there was one more piece of business standing between her and her fallen brother.

Rebekah grabbed the vinaya powder from Luc's other hand while Klaus twisted the stake free from Lisette's rib cage. "I *made* you, you stupid bastard," she hissed, throwing Luc back against a pile of Klaus's paintings, just a few feet from Tomás's corpse. "There's only one way for you to be free of me—and if you want it so badly, it's yours."

Suddenly Rebekah saw sunlight again, and heard the far-off laughter of her brothers as she chased them around the trees of Mystic Falls.

"Rebekah," Klaus called, and tossed her the White Oak stake. Her hand shot out to catch it.

"Rebekah," Luc began, but she didn't need to hear any more of what he had to say. New Orleans was burning, and in the morning things would start anew. There would be no place in that reborn city for Luc. He still had Lisette's blood on his hands, and his time was over.

Rebekah plunged the stake into Luc's chest, striking squarely for his heart, and then everything seemed to happen at once.

Luc's hand shot out, not to block the stake but to press Lisette's drying blood into the wall behind him. His hand reached Tomás's carved symbols, and they seemed to soak up the blood as if they were thirsty for more.

Klaus never used the fireplaces in the attic, and they contained no wood, yet all four of them burst to life with a roar. The sound was far too loud for the attic alone: It sounded as if every fireplace in the massive house had ignited at the same time. The fire burned the very air, and it ate into the stone of the chimneys surrounding it, spreading quickly toward the wooden walls.

Luc's body fell to the ground as the life edged out of him. His long blond hair tangled with Tomás's dark locks, their two profiles looked in opposite directions—like Janus, the god who looked toward the future and the past. Rebekah had had enough of gods for a good long while.

Somewhere behind her, Elijah rose to his feet. His face was drawn, and his brown eyes blazed with almost feverish strength. "The house will burn," he said. His voice was hoarse at first, but it began to clear as he spoke. Rebekah could almost see him growing stronger by the moment, shaking off the last traces of his curse. "Tomás used witchcraft, and we won't be able to stop it now."

Klaus clapped his brother on the back, his eyes suspiciously damp. Rebekah threw herself into Elijah's arms for just a moment, wanting to cry with the relief of seeing him well at last, but there wasn't time. Elijah was right, as usual: The fire was spreading fast.

"Kol's and Finn's coffins are in the east wing," Klaus said gruffly, stepping away to pull a few canvases from their stacks. He tossed them through the broken window, not bothering to check if they landed safely. "I'll go get them, and bring out whatever else I can find."

"I'll start with our books," Elijah added, "then work my way along the western rooms." He lifted Lisette gently, cradling her body as he followed Klaus to the staircase.

Rebekah pulled the stake from Luc's corpse, carefully closed his eyes with her hand. She took the pouch of vinaya powder from him as well, unwilling to leave him with any of the treasures he'd thought worthy of his betrayal.

The paintings behind him were already beginning to smolder, and the air inside the attic was nearly as smoky as the air outside.

There were a lot of things Rebekah wanted to take with her from the mansion, and she'd have to hurry if she wanted to save all of her possessions. But even if she only had a few minutes before the fire consumed everything, Rebekah knew every inch of her home. She moved more quickly than any fire.

So when she turned her back on Luc's corpse, it was because she had chosen to let him burn.

TWENTY-SEVEN

Elijah felt like he was submerged in dark water, his body slowly floating to the top of a great, salty lake. He could see two pale moons in the sky above him, and as he drifted upward the moons rippled and changed, dimming and twisting to become two faces.

Elijah opened his eyes as his face broke the surface, and saw Rebekah and Klaus leaning over him, anxiously waiting for him to stir. The eastern edge of the sky was light with the promise of dawn, and he wondered how long they had sat over him that way, worrying. After his long ordeal, Elijah had welcomed some real sleep, but it was clear that his siblings were relieved to see him conscious again.

Klaus and Rebekah had never looked more like siblings to Elijah than they did in that moment, with twin expressions of concern and terrible, painful love on their faces. Rebekah's hair was paler and Klaus's eyes had more green, but the shadows of the forest and the flames of the fire had washed their differences away. They might as well have been the two faces of Janus, except that both of them were turned toward the present moment.

"It's all right," Elijah told them, sitting up and brushing debris from his cloak. "I'm still cured."

"I should think so," Klaus said, leaning back and pretending he hadn't been worried. "Our dear sister here even killed an extra vampire for you, just to make sure. Our final count was one hundred and one, plus all the witches and werewolves. Not a bad pull for one night's work."

Privately, Elijah wondered if Klaus's count was really as accurate as he believed. The instant Luc died, Elijah's mind completely cleared of all his pain. The changes he'd felt were so momentous and so sudden that Elijah imagined some lucky vampire had managed to duck out of the warehouse just before it burst into a deadly inferno. Or perhaps it was more likely that the witches had gotten it wrong: that the number of deaths required was one hundred and one. With Amalia dead along with the rest of the fighters in the warehouse, they'd never know the real answer.

All Elijah knew for certain was that he was free from Alejandra at last.

"I'm sorry," he said, watching the smoke that still rose from the wreckage of their city and their home.

"For what?" asked Rebekah. "We're all to blame for what happened last night."

Most of New Orleans was in ruins, and Elijah guessed that they'd spent the rest of the night under the stars. It reminded him of their human lives, of those nights when they had snuck outside, whispering and giggling and feeling the promise of the world open up on every side.

"I should have understood that she was manipulating me. I lost my way, and I lost my faith in our family," he finally said.

"We'd all gone a bit astray," Rebekah reminded him, looking at Klaus. "The humans understood our weaknesses, and they told us the lies we were most ready to believe."

It wasn't lost on any of them that two of the worst of those lies had revolved around Klaus. Elijah had thought him a traitor, and Rebekah had been ready to seek revenge on him for a murder. The bonds between the three siblings were strong, but they were also twisted by a thousand doubts and complications that Elijah suspected they would ever truly untangle.

"The grudge I carried against the witches and werewolves blinded me," Klaus admitted, surprising Elijah. Perhaps New Orleans truly had been cleansed by a fire—and Klaus was ready to begin again. "In my hunger for revenge I lost sight of my family, and even of my own self. The humans may have exploited our weaknesses, but they didn't create them."

"We all could have been wiser," Elijah said, then closed his eyes against the fresh pain of losing Lisette.

"So the next time we will." Klaus shrugged. "There's plenty of space to rebuild, and I think an argument could be made that the surviving quarter of the city is the one that still belonged to us."

He flashed his charming, sardonic smile, and Elijah saw the beginning of a matching grin on Rebekah's lips. Together they had put down the human rebellion in New Orleans, and had dealt a huge blow to the strongholds of the werewolves and witches. It'd be a long time before those factions held power in their hands again, and in spite of the cost, that was a good night's work.

"One step at a time," Elijah said, rising to his feet and savoring how normal it felt to stand. He had almost forgotten the powerful, easy feel of his own body. He hadn't felt this well since before he had taken up with Alejandra, and the memory of *her* death brought him nothing but relief.

It was loyalty that held Elijah's world together, and he'd devoted himself to someone who wasn't worthy of his fidelity—who had never offered him the same thing in return. That realization was almost more painful than the physical torture she had inflicted on him.

"The sun will be up in a moment, and right now there is one more good-bye I must make," he said.

Rebekah bit her lip and Klaus looked down, but both of them fell in behind him, like an honor guard. They followed him to the ash-filled front lawn, where the great fountain still stood. Behind it, the bones of the mansion rose in strange, uneven shapes, pointing toward the sky like fingers on a corpse. And in the same spot where Klaus had wed Vivianne Lescheres, the Mikaelsons worked together to build a funeral pyre for Lisette.

They'd left her body fully covered, draped from head to toe in a shroud of thick black silk that shimmered like obsidian in the first rays of sunlight. From her bodice, Rebekah pulled out the pouch of vinaya powder and the White Oak stake. She laid one deadly object on either side of Lisette's lifeless form, like reminders of what the young vampire had died for.

"She died for *me*," Elijah said, and he felt his siblings look at him curiously.

"She saved you twice at the same time," Klaus remarked. "She would have been unbearably pleased to know that."

"Niklaus and I discussed it a little while you slept," Rebekah added. The rising sun shone in her golden hair, and made the ruins of the house behind her look older somehow, as if they were the remains of a civilization that had already been gone for centuries. "The powder has to burn, of course. Vinaya can't be allowed to exist, not in New Orleans or anywhere else we come across it. But we thought that you—and Lisette—would like to see the White Oak stake go up as well. As a symbol of our strength together, and our commitment to . . ."

She trailed off, looking at Klaus, who shrugged. "To not killing each other," he suggested, and even though Elijah could feel the sting of unshed tears in his eyes, he laughed.

"Good enough," he agreed. He steeled himself for the next part, when he would truly lose Lisette to the Other Side. He knew in his mind that she was already there, but his heart kept telling him that as long as he could see her body, he might be able to keep a piece of her with him always.

Elijah knew what Lisette would have said about

that. He owed it to her to let her rest in peace—she'd already put up with enough of his selfish ways.

He reached forward and grasped the edge of the shroud. He gave it one firm, fast pull, tugging it free of Lisette's body without disturbing the two sinister objects by her sides.

Sunlight struck Lisette's skin and began to burn her. She was lost in the flames within seconds, and the wood piled beneath her began to smoke as the fire caught. Soon, the stake and the vinaya were nothing but ashes, and the pyre burned high under the mercilessly blue sky.

"This is a new beginning for us," Elijah said at last. "We have suffered alone, but that suffering has brought us back together again." He reached to either side of him, taking Klaus's and Rebekah's hands in his. "This is how our family was meant to be," Elijah reminded his siblings. "Always and forever."

EPILOGUE

*A*lmost a month after the fire had burned out, Klaus could still smell soot on the evening air. Spring had come in earnest, with patches of bright green forcing their way up through the charred soil. New houses were rising everywhere, constructed from Spanish brick and iron—no longer wooden tinderboxes. Klaus doubted they would fare much better than the old wooden ones had, but he was amused by the humans' optimism. Who was he to say that something built in the middle of a vampire-owned swamp wouldn't last?

The Mikaelsons, by contrast, had been slow to rebuild. Klaus had lost his army and won his war in a single night, but the experience had left him more restless than triumphant. In one stroke he had defeated three enemies and put an end to his brother's curse, a victory so complete that it left nothing but silence in its wake. Yet silence and peace were more boring than so-called triumph had any right to be.

The faint, sweet smell of honeysuckle drifted toward him on the mild evening breeze, piercing the stale odor of old smoke and driving it away. Klaus slowed his steps a little, watching the sun grow and redden as it plunged toward the horizon.

The sound of hammers rang out around him, and he could hear mortar being scraped between stones. The work in the city would go on well into the night, now that New Orleans's residents were no longer afraid of the dark. The worst of the fearmonger had died in the fire, along with the creatures the humans had once barred their doors against.

It was as if the slate had been wiped clean, even for those who had no idea what had happened. The few surviving werewolves and witches had their suspicions, but no one seemed to have the heart for more war, not after the toll the great fire had taken. It was as if the entire city had silently agreed that enough was enough.

A small, dark-haired child hurtled around a corner and nearly bumped into Klaus, wheeling his arms backward with all his might to avoid contact. "Watch where you're going!" he piped shrilly, crossing his arms over his thin chest and puffing it out as best he could.

"That's good advice," Klaus agreed. "I suggest you take it yourself."

"This is *my* quarter," the boy explained. His bony wrists stuck out of his faded sleeves, and he couldn't have seen more than eight summers. But he had the imperious manner of a prince in disguise, and Klaus found himself more entertained than annoyed.

"What makes you think that, little gentleman?" he asked, glancing along the cobblestoned street before him. Werewolves had lived here once, Klaus realized. Now all that was left were the remnants of old French architecture and burnt-out shells that had yet to be demolished.

"My father built our house with his own two hands," the boy—the little werewolf—announced proudly. "And he was a hero in the fire; he died saving lots and lots of other people."

Klaus smiled unpleasantly, imagining how many similar stories were drifting through the city. It was a fairy tale so laughable that only a child would believe it. "And who told you that?" he asked.

"My mother," the puppy said. "She told me all about it."

"We have something in common, then," Klaus replied, bending down to meet the child's eyes. "My mother told me lies about my father, too."

The boy's head jerked back in surprise, as if Klaus had struck him. "My mother doesn't lie," he insisted. "Ignacio Guerrera was a great man, and if he hadn't run into the fire to help people, this whole *city* would have belonged to him someday. And I'm going to prove it. I'm going to be just like him when I grow up. You'll see."

That, Klaus decided, was a threat that could wait for another day. "*If* you grow up," Klaus corrected, feeling the little sting as his fangs extended. He bared them at the boy, adding a theatrical snarl for good measure.

The werewolf child screamed and ran, his thin shoes slapping against the cobblestones as he vanished down a side street. Klaus watched him go, amused. He did have a soft spot for children, even if he never expected to have any of his own.

His wandering took him back toward the river. No one had been saved from the warehouse; he was sure of that. The fire had leveled the entire district, and all that was left of Tomás's warehouse was scorched ground, a mountain of ash, and the larger bones of the human skeleton that were too big to burn. The spilled rum had burned hot and fast, and the vampires must have gone up like so many dry torches. There would have been no chance to think or to plan; no escape from the inferno that raged everywhere.

The fact that Klaus hadn't heard the slightest whisper of revenge only confirmed that no one had survived. Everyone supposedly knew *someone* who had miraculously escaped the blaze, yet no one had come forward to breathe a word about how it had started.

The Guerrera boy would realize the truth someday, Klaus imagined, and then there would be one more disillusioned werewolf roaming the streets of New Orleans. But there would always be another dispute to settle, another cause to fight for. That was just the way the world was for Klaus.

There was only one place in the entire city that Klaus missed. The Southern Spot had burned along with everything else. Klaus hadn't decided yet what he would build on that lot—whether he would improve the structure that had been there before, create something completely different, or simply leave it for some eager developer to swallow up. There should have been plenty of land to go around, but in the free-for-all that had followed the destruction, there was always someone with an eye out for more.

The scent of honeysuckle came to him again, nearer

this time. Klaus's steps turned toward it as if of their own accord. He followed it past villas and hovels and piles of charred rubble. The darkening sky was quickly filling with stars.

Klaus turned a corner that felt vaguely familiar, and at the far end of the street he saw a young woman walking alone. Even for the new, safer New Orleans, that seemed unusually bold, and boldness had always caught his eye.

She might have been about twenty, in a gauzy white dress that left her white arms bare to the warm night. Her long black hair tumbled loose around her shoulders, and to Klaus it seemed she must have stolen out of her bed, unnoticed by the family who surely thought she was asleep.

He almost called to her. She looked so familiar standing there that he believed for a moment they were old friends. But Klaus's friends had short life spans, and as of late, they left more quickly than they came.

The girl turned as if she had heard him approach, and the spray of lilacs that climbed the brick wall behind her framed her face like a soft purple halo. "Is someone there?" she called, perhaps out of habit, since he knew that she could see him. The moon was nearly full again and the night was bright.

"You shouldn't be out alone after dark," Klaus

warned her, locking his eyes on to hers as he drew closer. Her eyes were blacker than the evening sky, like pieces of onyx set into her lovely face. Her mouth was a curious red slash, and twisted into a knowing smile. She almost looked like someone he had once known.

"I'm hardly the only one out here," she said, raising one black eyebrow. Her voice was low and soft, and he could hear refinement and education in it. She had been bred for an ambitious marriage, no doubt, and sheltered from even a hint of scandal for her entire life. She couldn't possibly have any idea how vulnerable she truly was just then. "I wanted to watch the stones being laid for our new house, but Mama believes that seeing our old home will bring me too much pain. I think that's just silly."

"The workers will be using torchlight by now," Klaus guessed. There was something so familiar about her, but Klaus wasn't feeling especially nostalgic at the moment. He only felt hungry. Just looking at her made his fangs extend. "I'd be happy to escort you there, if you tell me the way."

Her eyes widened in delight, and she took a few eager steps toward him. "Would you?" she asked. "You're too kind, sir."

"So I'm often told," Klaus agreed, holding out his arm politely.

The young woman lightly placed her hand on his forearm, falling in beside him as if they were old friends. After they had walked down the street, Klaus turned them down a darker alleyway.

"I'm sorry, sir, but my home is the other way."

"Ah, señorita, my apologies," he murmured, then pulled her in by her waist and slipped his other hand over her mouth so that she couldn't scream. For just a moment, he showed her his true face before sinking his fangs into her throat. He wanted her to know who it was who killed her, to be afraid before she died.

Her blood tasted of lilacs and honey, so young and sweet that Klaus's mouth worked to extract every last drop. He could feel her heart flutter and slow, and he knew that she could no longer scream, even if she wanted to.

The girl died where she stood, still resting one hand on his arm, but the trusting look in her eyes had been replaced by one of horror. Klaus hid her corpse in a burnt-out shop—it had been a butcher's counter once, he realized with some amusement.

Feeling even better than before, he stuck his hands into his pockets and continued on his way, enjoying the caress of the warm evening air on his face. New Orleans had never seemed so full of possibilities.

Keep reading for a sneak peek at the script where it
all began . . . the pilot episode of *The Originals*!

the Vampire Diaries

the Vampire Diaries

Episode #420

#2J6670

"The Originals"

Written by Julie Plec

Based on the novel by L. J. Smith

Directed by Chris Grismer

Production Draft   2/22/13

3, 3A, 5, 6, 6A, 7, 9, 17, 18, 19, 20, 22, 24, 25, 27, 28, 30, 31, 33, 35, 36, 38, 41, 41A, 42, 46

Added Sc. 23A outside cemetery & Sc. 37A Ext. City of the Dead

Note 2 page addendum at the end

EXT.
NEW ORLEANS -
JACKSON SQUARE - NIGHT 31

Klaus makes his way into Jackson
Square. He takes a seat on a bench,
staring up at the cathedral. A long
beat -

                    KLAUS
          Are you here to give me
          another pep talk about
          the joys of fatherhood?

REVEAL Elijah has sat down next to
him.

                    ELIJAH
          I've said everything I
          need to say.

A beat as they sit there in silence.

KLAUS

I forgot how much I liked
this town. We were happy
here.

ELIJAH

I didn't forget. All
these centuries we've
spent together and yet I
can mark the times our
family has been truly
happy on one hand. I
hated to leave it.

KLAUS

As did I.

ELIJAH

You know the witches
can't leave. They
practice ancestral magic,
drawing power directly
from their dead in those
cemeteries. If they go,
they leave the source of
their power behind.

                    KLAUS
        I suppose that explains
        their hunger for
        revolution. That, and I
        believe Marcel has found
        some means of controlling
        them. I want to know what
        it is.

Elijah can sense that something has
shifted, he just doesn't know what.

                    ELIJAH
        What's on your mind,
        brother?

                    KLAUS
        For a thousand years I
        lived in fear. Every time
        I settled anywhere, our
        father found me, chased
        me off. He made me feel
        powerless. I hated that.
                (then)
        This town was my home
        once. And in my absence,

Marcel has gotten
everything I ever wanted.
Power. Loyalty. Family. I
made him in my image, and
he has bettered me.
        (then)
I want it back. I want to
be its king.

Elijah dares to hope.

                ELIJAH
And what of Hayley and
the baby?

A long beat, then . . .

                KLAUS
Every kind needs an heir.
Tell Sophie Deveraux we
have a deal.

                END OF ACT FIVE

*J*ulie Plec skillfully juggles work in film and television as both a producer and a writer. She is the co-creator and executive producer of *The Vampire Diaries* and the creator of *The Vampire Diaries* spin-off, *The Originals*, which tells the story of history's first vampire family.

Plec got her start as a television writer on the ABC Family series *Kyle XY*, which she also produced for its three-year run. She also collaborated with Greg Berlanti and Phil Klemmer on the CW drama *The Tomorrow People*, the story of a small group of people gifted with extraordinary paranormal abilities.

Julie wrote a screenplay adaptation of *The Tiger's Curse*, which has Ineffable Pictures and Lotus Entertainment attached to produce, with Shekhar Kapur directing. She will also produce the feature *@emma* with Darko Entertainment. Past feature production credits include *Scream 2* and *Scream 3*, Greg Berlanti's *Broken Hearts Club*, Wes Craven's *Cursed*, and *The Breed*.

Thirsty for some Blood?

The *Vampire Diaries* seasons 1-5 now available
on DVD, Blu-ray™ and Digital HD.
Look for the new season on Digital HD.

Craving More?

See where it all began...
The Originals: The Complete First Season
on DVD, Blu-ray™ and on Digital HD.